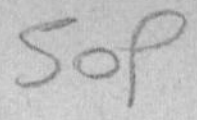

Penguin Books
Somebody's Sister

Derek Marlowe was bo
was sent down from Lo
controversial article in hi
for a while took up actin
The Seven Who Were Ha
performed at the Edinburg
transferred to the Royal Co
1961. This won the Foyle Av
Play of that year. In 1962 he *ower Depths* for the Royal Shakespeare Company. Two years later he went to Berlin on a Ford Foundation Grant and wrote two plays which were performed there and at the Questors Theatre. He also won an American 'Emmy' for the television series, *The Search For the Nile*. In 1965 he wrote *A Dandy in Aspic*, which achieved immediate success. It has been published in fifteen countries and made into a film (with Laurence Harvey and Mia Farrow) for which he wrote the screenplay. His other novels include *The Memoirs of a Venus Lackey* (1968), *A Single Summer With L.B.* (1969), *Echoes of Celandine* (1970; reissued and filmed as *The Disappearance*), *Do You Remember England?* (1972) and *Nightshade* (1976).

Derek Marlowe

Somebody's Sister

Penguin Books

Penguin Books Ltd, Harmondsworth,
Middlesex, England
Penguin Books, 625 Madison Avenue,
New York, New York 10022, U.S.A.
Penguin Books Australia Ltd, Ringwood,
Victoria, Australia
Penguin Books Canada Ltd, 2801 John Street,
Markham, Ontario, Canada L3R 1B4
Penguin Books (N.Z.) Ltd, 182–190 Wairau Road,
Auckland 10, New Zealand

First published by Jonathan Cape 1974
Published in Penguin Books 1977

Made and printed in Great Britain by
Hazell Watson & Viney Ltd,
Aylesbury, Bucks
Set in Linotype Granjon

To Herb Caen

Saturday

Overture

The screen before her now began to present its own images – some familiar, some distorted, some out of focus, like a series of colour transparencies projected at random from an alien machine; blurring, converging (a rectangle of red and black, an obelisk of freckles along the nose), a rapid conveyor belt of abstracts, difficult to identify (a light bulb or is it a moon?), a strobeing of views, pulsating before the eyes, clicking on and off, blurring again, swivelling, reversing, freezing for a moment upside down, then the frame is steady and she can see (what *do* they call them? Rivets?) she can see rivets and even begin to count them before there is another slide, another transparency.

She becomes aware of the noise, seemingly very close, a personal soundtrack to her vision, but her ears cannot register the details. Colours blind, a musical honky-tonk underscores the fractured sights, then the spool begins to splay out, sprockets snap, the film tears and the screen becomes a child's kaleidoscope of prisms, a sudden cascade of rivulets and lace, tributaries of patterns, irreplaceable jigsaw pieces – and then suddenly there is fresh air and she can see where she is. *Now* she knows. She worries naturally about her dress as she hears it tear, hears the splintering, hears the music, feels the bonnet (such an absurd word), feels it caress her (*When I was a child I could stand on my head for five and a half minutes and I bet* you *can't*), and then the celluloid finally, inevitably, rips from its moorings and snaps, and the wheel spins aimlessly and comes to rest. As does the girl. Or what is left of her. On the Golden Gate Bridge. At five in the morning.

Naturally there are other cars. Some of them even slow down when the drivers realize that the dead body impaled between metal girders and decorated with sequins of glass is that of a young girl. But they don't stop. Not on the bridge. That, for those familiar with the statute books, would be illegal.

Except, of course, if you are a witness.

I

In a rooming-house a mile north of Alemany Boulevard, San Francisco, and west of Mission Street, a man is dressed in blue boxer-shorts and nothing else. He is shaving with a Gillette safety-razor (the unfashionable model composed of three separate parts), shaving very carefully and following a pattern that has been developed, with a few minor deviations, over approximately thirty-five years. That is to say, the razor commences its short itinerary parallel to the base of the left ear and completes its tour above the upper lip before being rinsed, dried and placed on the left-hand corner of a shelf. It is doubtful, of course, whether the man is conscious of the uniform monotony of such an act, for it is of a trivial nature and he is preoccupied by something else. The refrain of a popular song has been teasing his memory since he awoke, but the title still eludes him. He has retraced from bed to shower to sink each action of the previous day, revisiting bars, replaying yesterday's music on the car radio, and he will continue to do so long after you or I would have abandoned the search until the title fingersnaps in his mind and he can relax. Details such as this are important to him: the tics, the gestures, the petty mannerisms we all take for granted, are noted and filed away, for they have not only helped the man to earn a living, they have also kept him alive.

The room itself, like its occupant, is unremarkable in appearance. The colour of the walls is, or rather *was*, Burnt Sienna. So too is the ceiling, though the brown there is lighter and more uneven, relying on the position of the ashtrays for its texture. There are three ashtrays – one on the arm of a chair, a second by the sink, and the third on the desk by the window. It (the third ashtray, pale green and white) bears the motif of *The Garden of Allah*, and no doubt could be classified as a souvenir if one were to speculate from what dead and famous mouths it once claimed its contents. But that would be a meaningless pastime, for there is nothing in the room to expose its anachronism. The desk, the telephone, the furniture, even the faded notepad, are all its contemporaries, having played their individual roles in the man's life for a quarter of a century, though that phrase would startle him. It is misleading, implying a hibernation on his part. A standing-still, and this, in truth, was not exactly so. There *had* been achievements over the past three decades (unorthodox achievements if you wish, but achievements nevertheless), and there had been rewards as well. That, at least, cannot be denied.

If questioned about his profession, and the man was in a favourable mood, he would probably point to a filing cabinet in the corner of the room, unlock a drawer and reveal the rows of folders, each one neatly arranged in alphabetical order, and each one, in turn, recording a brief summary of a few weeks in someone else's life. The names, unless they were yours, would probably mean nothing, for they are not celebrated in any way, except perhaps to past readers of the city's newspapers and occasionally to the State Police. All that could be said was that the subjects were either adulterous, missing or dead, and that the great majority of these incidents occurred before the year 1964. If there is any significance in why the years since then had been so barren (at least as far as the filing cabinet revealed), it would not be mentioned by the man. That, to him, was just the way things were and he would simply relock the drawer and return to his own personal routine of the day. And at nine fifteen in the morning, it was shaving.

We have overlooked only two objects that might be of interest. They are photographs and are framed on the wall to the right of the desk. The first is of a woman. She is not pretty in the conventional sense, nor in her pose does she claim to be. Without meeting her, one feels one would like her and even confide in her. The unselfish face of someone one neglects until it is too late and resolutions become guilt. It is inscribed: *To Walter, with love as ever, Dorothy, Christmas 1961.*

Below, in a larger frame, is a flash ight photograph taken, as would be noted by the observant eye, in this very room. Two men, both in double-breasted suits, smiling into camera with a look of almost infantile pride as they hold up an office sign: BRACKETT AND KEMBLE.

The man shaving is Brackett.

He is, to be precise, Walter (*never* Wally) Brackett, and is, as far as is known, no relation to the famous Charles Brackett, the writer. In fact, he is no relation to anyone at present, except to those American cousins who insist on being removed three or four times each generation, usually to St Paul, Minnesota. Brackett himself is English, having been born in Surrey when people wanted to be born in Surrey, but left the country for ever after the Second World War simply because he was bored. Originally, he had planned to travel to Africa (the map of the Continent was very pink in those days. As were the landlords) but he had changed his mind halfway for no apparent reason and taken the first boat out of Lisbon. When it finally reached its destination, Brackett found himself in San Francisco, saw no reason to dislike the town and has been there ever since.

He is now fifty-three years old and looks it. This is not due to a misspent youth or even a misspent middle-age, but simply because he has the features and temperament that take the years as they come without a backward glance, and the result, consequently, is not unattractive. His hair may be thinning above the temples, his waistline thickening, but Brackett is not a vain man, like so many of his contemporaries who try to keep themselves 'in trim'. If there is a choice of an elevator or the stairs, he will take the elevator, even for two flights, for he decided long ago that any form of deliberate exercise (isometrics, squash, press-ups, that kind of thing) was not only time-consuming but also somewhat absurd. In an age where heroes look as though the referee has just counted ten, Brackett at a hundred and eighty pounds of Southern Comfort and broken bones would never be unimpressive – whether it be in a downtown bar or on the neighbour's croquet lawn. Somebody had once said unkindly that his face looked like a soufflé after the oven door had been opened too early.

It is now nine twenty-five and today is the day he visits Kemble. But he is in no hurry. He takes his time as he moves from the sink and crosses towards a dark mahogany wardrobe.

From a drawer, he takes a white shirt and removes it from its plastic envelope. He doesn't *select* the shirt, for it is the only clean one he possesses; but it is a good shirt by any standard, hand-stitched, and betrays its age only in its style. It complements the double-breasted suit with ease. A plain blue tie, a pair of Oxford brogues and Brackett is almost ready. The song however still irritates him and he stands, arms folded, gazing abstractedly at his reflection in the mirror. A broad forehead above a deceptively straight nose – it had been broken twice, but reset with care in 1951 and 1956. Grey eyes, and a mouth that had once reminded a woman of John Garfield. *'John who?' 'Garfield, honey. You know, "Body and Soul".'*

If Brackett were honest with himself, he would have had to admit that he liked seeing Kemble less and less. Not that his affection for his partner had diminished in any way, but simply because he had found that the regular weekly encounters had begun to distress him to such an extent that he was finding it impossible to disguise the fact.

Once (too many years ago now) the visits had been exciting; the two men had planned for the day when Kemble would leave the Rest Home (*Autumn Glades*) and it would be BRACKETT AND KEMBLE once more, as if nothing had ever changed. But that day had still not arrived and Brackett was convinced it never would. The talk between them indicated that all too well as it slowly declined through the seasons from optimism to banalities, declining as imperceptibly as leaves abandoning a tree until suddenly every branch and twig was exposed and he saw Kemble as he really was: a man prematurely retired, sitting on a patio reading comics and waiting to die. That was the sum of it and Brackett hated it. He hated staring at the pathetic creatures on the Hoovered lawns being wheeled around with blankets over their knees, or being carried out with sheets over their heads. But today he would go again and arrive on time, play his part (he was adept at that. The smile, the jokes. The lies) and then he would leave on time because you know, Harry, what the traffic is like in this town.

Brackett took the keys from the desk-drawer and stared for a moment at the gun, a Police Special, lying amid a nest of paperclips and staples. He even picked it up for a moment, surprised how cold it was, then suddenly slammed it back into the darkness of the drawer as if it were an obscene creature he had mistakenly tempted into the light, and hurried out of the room to the delicatessen below without looking back.

It was known as Fatty's. This is not, as one might expect, a reflection on the size of the owner (a diminutive Hungarian called Liebermann who had been born just west of the Danube on Ellis Island, New York), but due to an apocryphal legend that the actor Roscoe 'Fatty' Arbuckle had visited the delicatessen on the eve of his notorious soirée in Room 1227 of the St Francis Hotel. As if to substantiate the myth, a framed portrait of the comedian used to hang beneath the liverwurst, but was removed, it is rumoured, by an earnest young representative of the Coca-Cola Bottling Company and replaced by the Petty Calendar for 1942. Frankly, no one believed a word of it but, in its way, it added some dubious glamour to the grime of the shop, whose customers could be counted on a fork. Brackett, more out of necessity than choice, was one of them.

The package was waiting for him on the counter as it always was each Saturday morning. He picked it up and thanked the Hungarian and began to walk towards the door.

'Don't forget to give my best to Mr Kemble,' Liebermann called after him.

'I always do that, Mr Liebermann.'

There may be trouble ahead, but while there's moonlight and music and love and rom– No, that wasn't it.

Brackett walked past the cartons and crates, the jilted Petty girl still on the wall, and out into the street to his car. It wasn't his favourite street in San Francisco, but then nor was Nob Hill. It just happened to be the street he lived on; he knew the people and the bars and the sounds at night. He was known there, for what it was worth, and that wasn't much anymore. Even Brackett had to admit to that when the light was out and the sleeping tablets failed to work. His wife once said he was a proud man and Brackett had agreed, adding that he was proud of being proud. It was a small joke but he meant it. Without that pride (a mixture of tenacity and the creed of Micawber) he knew that in the years alone, when Kemble and Dorothy were no longer with him, he would never have survived. That he would have cracked somehow; not through alcohol or drugs or even remorse, but simply out of the realization that he no longer belonged.

As he drove away, he selected some music on the car radio, found something by Cole Porter and left it at that. He didn't glance in the rear-view mirror until he was at Mission Street, but if he had he would have seen the police car. He would have seen it stop outside the delicatessen and he would have seen the doors open. But Brackett's mind was elsewhere. He had remembered a bar between Valley and Twenty-Ninth that he had once known well. No dancers, none of that bump and grind. Just peace and a low light. And a single drink before he met Kemble. That's all.

Ten to one, he thought, they've pulled it down.

2

'I thought there'd be a *Batman* this week. There should have been a *Batman* this week, Walter. There's a *Sgt Rock*, but he's not the same since Kubert stopped drawing him. I have nothing against Russ Heath but he's not the same as Kubert. Kubert really knew how to draw. *Silver Surfer*? Well, that's fine ... I suppose. I'm not saying I like him but it's fine. But it's a pity about Kubert. He was an artist, Walter. He should never have stopped drawing *Sgt Rock*. It isn't the same...'

Brackett didn't reply, but sat on the neighbouring wicker chair and studied Kemble as he sorted through the comics, taking each one in turn from the package and laying it carefully aside.

'*Young Love*?' Kemble said with surprise, holding up a magazine. 'Since when did Peter Liebermann start reading *Young Love*?'

'Pete's in college, Harry. These are Sarah's comic books.'

'Sarah Liebermann? Is Sarah Liebermann reading now?'

'She's twelve years old.'

'Sarah is *twelve*?'

'I told you she was.'

'She's twelve now? I never knew that. Twelve. Well, I never knew that.'

'They grow up fast.'

'Fast. And reading. But *Young Love*, Walter. She's reading *that*? In another two years she'll be dangerous. Believe me, Walter. Those kind of girls.'

Brackett leant back and stared across the lawns and the golf-links beyond and the Pacific beyond that. An old man sitting in a golf-cart waved towards the patio but Brackett ignored him.

'How are you feeling, Harry?'

'Maybe I could exchange this for one of those *Detective Comics*. I could do that. Don't you think, Walter?'

'You look well. You really do.'

Kemble glanced at him, then turned away shyly, clutching the package in his hands, liver-spots showing on the skin.

'You know what you told me last week?' he said finally.

'What was that? '

'About nobody calling anyone "Blue-eyes" any more?'

'Did I say that?'

'Well, I've been thinking. Maybe it's time you took stock of your life, Walter.'

'I'm all right.'

'Do you know what I mean?'

'I'm only fifty-three.'

'And in ten years – look at Sarah Liebermann. Thirteen years old already.'

'Twelve.'

'Just like that. You wake up one morning and a decade has passed you by.'

'I'm all right.'

Silence. In a room above them someone was playing a record by Johnny Mathis. Then Brackett heard Kemble's voice, nervous, almost apologetic:

'Do ... do people still come to see us, Walter? *Clients?*'

'Sure they do. I told you that –'

'When did you tell me that?'

'I told you that. Last week, a woman asked me to find her husband.'

Kemble suddenly smiled:

'Alimony, eh? Well, we can handle that. Came to us last week eh?'

'Sunday.'

'I was going to say it would be a Sunday. You notice it's always a Sunday. Wife sees the empty chair, sees the kids in the house. It's always Sunday for alimony. You find him?'

Brackett shook his head, not out of failure but to give him time to think of a reply. In the end, he decided to say nothing. Kemble would forget.

'I'd better leave now, Harry. You know what the traffic is like in this town.'

'Doctor said I'd be my old self again soon.'

'*Yoang* self.'

'*Young* self. Yes. I'll tell him that. That's what I'll say to him. Young self.'

'You can afford to, Harry.'

As Brackett stood up and picked up his hat, Kemble suddenly leant forward and took his arm.

'Walter?'

'Yes?'

There was a silence again and Brackett looked down at his partner's face. He saw the eyes, the tiredness that had invaded the body like termites into wood. The scars were everywhere.

'Walter... I dreamt about Dorothy again last night.'

A pause and then Kemble mumbled, 'I'm sorry,' and moved away as Brackett walked down the steps of the patio on to the grass.

'Good-bye, Harry. I'll see you next Saturday. Same time.'

He crossed the lawn towards the gates, feeling as conspicuous as a pyramid. He told himself not to look back but inevitably he did, and saw Kemble sitting in his chair, his arms crossed over his chest, head lowered almost in penance. One of the comic-books had dropped to the floor and was fluttering its pages at Kemble's feet like an irritating insect.

Brackett looked away, banishing his eyes from the building, the nurses, the wheelchairs, the smell of decay, and vowed once again never to return. It was then that he heard someone approach him and say:

'Your name Walter Brackett?'

He looked up, his eyes dazzled by the sun.

'Yes.'

'We'd like you to identify someone for us.'

Brackett focused on the uniform, then at the man. At the gates he saw the police car.

'Who?' he asked, confused.

'You tell us. You got a car?'

'Yes. It's –'

'Just follow us.'

'Where to?'

'The morgue. You know it?'

'At Central?'

'That's the one. You been there before?'

'Yes,' Brackett said quietly. 'I've been there before.'

On the patio, Kemble had looked up and was watching the two men walk towards the gates; then he picked up the comic and carefully straightened out each page before opening it, placing it on his lap, and began to read. It was *Green Lantern*. Number 85. Artwork by Adams.

A Fine Romance. Brackett almost jumped the lights, but that's what it was. He relaxed. *A Fine Romance*. Of course.

The morgue was to the left of the car-park and behind a border of rose bushes that needed pruning.

'What makes you think *I* can help?' Brackett asked.

'She had your card.'

'*She?*'

'That's all she had. Just your card.'

'Brackett and Kemble?'

'I never read it. I was just told to pick you up.'

The outside door didn't lead directly into the morgue, presumably so as not to offend anyone who might wander in by chance. But even if they had, they would discover nothing to depress them, except the paintwork. The visitor would simply find himself in a form of waiting-room, brightly lit and impartial; he would see two doors, perhaps, forbidding him to enter, a long desk, and behind that a desk-sergeant in shirt sleeves who would smile and ask him his name and advise him not to smoke. At Central, the desk-sergeant was called Henderson and looked like a B-movie version of the tough-but-honest cop. But then, as Brackett observed over the years, *all* American police looked like that, as if nature was deliberately trying to imitate art. Inferior art, perhaps, but that didn't diminish the analogy.

He was introduced to Henderson, who looked him over quickly as if assessing whether Brackett would become hysterical or faint when confronted by a corpse, decided that the odds were against it and led him towards one of the doors.

'Sorry to bring you all this way, Mr Brackett.'

'It wasn't far.'

'You been in a morgue before?'

'I thought I'd been *here* but it doesn't look the same.'

'Modernization,' the sergeant replied. 'What do you think of it?'

'To be honest, I don't think it matters.'

'For the stiffs, maybe not. But for the people who work here, it was unhealthy. Know what I mean?'

Brackett nodded apathetically and followed Henderson through the door until he was standing before a glass partition. To the right he could see three or four long tables, above which a microphone hung suspended from a cord. A row of sinks, bundles of rags, rubber aprons, a neat range of scientific cutlery, and a pin-up of Raquel Welch thumb-tacked to a wall.

'You from England?' Henderson asked.

'I was born there.'

A gulley was being pushed towards them by a porter. On the gulley was a body covered by a sheet.

'I took my wife to England once. Just for a week. We visited Brighton. You ever been to Brighton? That's on the sea.'

'No.'

'They have this Chinese Palace there. You know that?'

'You mean the Pavilion,' Brackett said, watching the gulley stop on the far side of the glass screen. He suddenly became impatient to know who the corpse was, not out of fear that he might see the face of a loved one (there wasn't any and that was that), but simply out of curiosity. They had said it was a woman and that she had his card. The natural assumption then was that it was a client, except that he hadn't had a client he could write to anyone's home about for five years, despite what he told Kemble.

'Is that what they call it? A Pavilion?' Henderson was saying. Brackett glanced at him, then said:

'Can I see her now?'

'What? Oh, sure.'

He nodded to the porter and the sheet was pulled away discreetly to the girl's shoulders. Brackett stared at the face, at the freckles, the delicately shaped mouth. He wanted to remove a wisp of hair from across her eyes. He didn't, surprisingly, notice the lacerations across the cheeks and forehead, the broken nose, for they seemed superfluous. He just looked at the face of a very beautiful girl and it sickened him. Not just because she was dead, but because no one even knew her name.

'How did she die?' Brackett asked.

'Car smash. Golden Gate Bridge. Wham! Report says she was on acid.'

'Acid?'

'Yeh. Acid. Drugs. Happens all the time.'

Brackett studied the girl's shoulders (she was no more than fourteen or fifteen), then once again at her hair. Blonde. It was odd but he had never really been attracted by blondes. It seemed almost a crime to admit it, in California of all places. Perhaps it was because there was something overtly sexual about blonde women. He had once discussed this with Kemble and he remembered Kemble smiling and reminding him that Dorothy had been blonde. But somehow that didn't seem the same thing at the time.

'Do you know her?' Henderson asked.

'I think her name is Mary Malewski,' Brackett replied.

'That's not good enough. We need a positive identification.'

'I know. But I'll have to look up my office files.'

'She a client of yours?'

'She visited me once. Told me she came here in ... oh, I don't know. It was last May sometime.'

Brackett walked towards the door.

'I'll call you from the office. If it is the same girl, I'll have an address on file. It might help.'

'If it'll help us to get her out of here, it will.'

'I'm sure her name's Malewski.'

'You got any kids, Brackett?'

'No.'

'Count yourself lucky. You know what my son wants to be?'

'I'd hate to ask.'

'Nothing. That's what he wants to be. Nothing.'

Brackett began to open the door into the waiting-room when Henderson stopped him and moved closer.

'You're one of those private investigators, aren't you?'

There was no need for Brackett to reply. He recognized the tone and had heard the follow-up before.

'Well, nothing personal, Brackett, but I think your job stinks.

To me you're just a hustler. A fucking hustler. That's my opinion. A rich fucking hustler.'

Brackett glanced back at the girl. An overhead fan had disturbed the wisp of hair so that it flickered over her mouth, almost as if she was breathing.

'I'll call you as soon as I reach the office,' he said, moving out towards the desk.

It was then that he saw Loomis. He didn't know that that was his name (he was to learn that soon), nor had he ever seen the man before. In fact he knew nothing about Loomis whatsoever, for if he had he would have driven away as fast as the speed limit would allow.

But Brackett, like all of us, was not blessed by foresight or prevision. He could only see what was before him and in Loomis he saw something that he had only witnessed once before. It was not simply nervousness as it appeared on the surface. It was more than that. Loomis, Brackett sensed immediately, was suffocating from stark, simple terror – the terror of someone who doesn't suspect but knows that at any moment he is going to be killed. It was as clear as that. And so Brackett stayed at the desk and stared at the man and waited for an opportunity to talk. It was, of course, the biggest mistake he would make in his life.

3

'Who's that?' Brackett asked.

The desk sergeant glanced at Loomis with an expression of irritated despair, as if he were another body that had been scraped up from the highway, brought in, weighed and dumped on his lap. One almost expected him to answer the question by reading a label tied round the man's toe.

'Witness,' he replied.

'To the girl?'

'Saw the whole thing.'

'Driver?'

'Pedestrian.'

'Pedestrian?' Brackett said, amazed. 'On the Golden Gate Bridge? When did it happen?'

'Who knows? Four, four-thirty this morning.'

'And he was walking?'

'Gave a statement. Jesus, you ought to see that statement.'

'Am I allowed to?'

'No.'

If Loomis heard the conversation, he made no reaction, but sat staring at the door as if posing for a seaside silhouette. It allowed Brackett time to observe his physical appearance, and what he observed was disappointing. Naturally there were personal details: a gold ring on the left hand, plain oval cuff-links, shoes that had been polished daily, a lightweight suit that was probably off the peg, a shirt cut from sea-island cotton. But these were mere appendices to a type, not to an individual, and, as Brackett was well aware, if you begin with an individual you *may* end up with a type. But begin with a type and you end up with nothing. Rich Boy or not, the figure sitting by the door was not giving away a thing. Except one. This very negation of his personality was no mere whim to conform to a class or a status. It was a calculated effort to be forgettable in the surroundings he chose to move in, and that, to Brackett, was the curiosity. He was airline lounge and cocktail bar and the man buying *Time* magazine at the Hilton. He was a credit-card and manicure and he knew it. Every step of the way. He was also scared.

'What's his name?' Brackett asked quietly.

'Loomis,' replied Henderson, glancing at the statement.

'Has he got a record?'

'Who knows?'

'Well, is he under arrest?'

'Christ no. He's just a witness. I told you. He volunteered a statement.'

'Then why are you holding him?' Brackett asked.

'Holding him!' Henderson shouted in the direction of the door. '*Who's* holding him? We've been trying to get rid of him since dawn but he won't go.'

'Why not?'

'Because he wants to leave by an official car, that's why.'

'So you told him this wasn't the Yellow Cab Company.'

'So I told him this wasn't the –'

Brackett smiled and walked across to Loomis.

'Mr Loomis? There's a car outside now. I'll drive you home.'

There was no reaction.

'It's just outside the door,' Brackett continued casually. 'I'm sorry it's not a squad car but they're not allowed to carry passengers unless they're in custody. You're not in custody, Mr Loomis.'

There was still no reaction. Brackett knew that he had been heard and that it was useless to say any more. He had lost and that was it. If Loomis had problems (and there was no question about that), he was keeping them to himself. The only thing to do was leave. There was the door and Brackett opened it.

'She was so young.'

Brackett stopped and looked down at Loomis. The head had turned slightly and he could now see the eyes, deep set under fine eyebrows. A semitic nose, heavy lower lips.

'She was just so young.'

The voice was steady. A slight accent that was probably from Kentucky. That wasn't a remarkable deduction. It was just that Dorothy had come from Kentucky.

'Who was so young?' Brackett asked quietly, moving closer to the bench.

'Pretty little dress . . . all torn. Pretty little dress. Shoe missing. I couldn't find the shoe. I looked in the back seat. I made a point of that. In the back seat. I . . . but you mustn't think that odd. It wasn't odd. You'll see that it wasn't odd. Not for us. Bizarre. Is that a word? *Harpers Bizarre*. Do you remember that joke?'

Brackett didn't answer but glanced across at Henderson and saw that he was occupied typing up a report. Suddenly Loomis said:

'Have you ever seen anyone killed?'

The question was directed at Brackett and he hesitated, then answered:

'Once or twice.'

'What did you see?'

'The end of a life. That's all.'

'No! Oh no.' Loomis's voice began to rise emphatically. 'Not the end of a life. But death. "Oh, please don't go round Union Square, Baby. I hate those palm trees." Death, that little girl. . .'

Brackett saw the desk-sergeant turn his head and stare at Loomis, then look at Brackett.

'What fucking palm trees?' Henderson called out but Brackett ignored him and sat down on the bench, leaning close to Loomis.

'Did you know the girl, Mr Loomis?'

'Know her?'

'Yes. Did you know her at all?'

'I told the sergeant I didn't.'

Brackett stared at Loomis, stared at the fear in the eyes, and said nothing.

'I saw her,' Loomis continued, retreating once more into his own entity. 'I was . . . standing and I just saw her and then I looked at her face. I saw her die. I saw her taken away from us.

Her dying ... it was just ... you mustn't laugh ... it was just like she was playing truant from the world. Do you understand what I mean? Like Huckleberry Finn. She just lit out. No light any more. Playing hookey from us all. You do understand, don't you?'

'Of course I do,' Brackett said. 'That's why you didn't jump, isn't it? Because you saw the girl?'

Brackett heard a slight gasp and Loomis turned away and was silent.

'Mr Loomis, let me take you home.'

There was no movement. Brackett opened his wallet and took out a card and placed it in Loomis's hand.

'There's my card. My name's Walter Brackett –'

But Loomis had already read the card and was staring up with an expression on his face that prompted Brackett to ask:

'Do you know me?'

Loomis was about to speak, then slowly shook his head. Brackett studied him, realized that nothing more could be achieved here, and said:

'Mr Loomis, I'm leaving now. If you have no objections to '62 Buicks, there's one on the other side of the door. It'll be there for two minutes, so I'll see you outside. Good-bye.'

There is no fixed pattern to a series of events. Nothing is predestined, no matter what philosophy or religion one adopts. Events are simply dealt out to each of us and we discard or accept them as they fall. The astrologist or the god or the psychiatrist may hand out guidance on a silver platitude, but it is a weak man who entrusts his life to such puerile navigation. This may not be your philosophy of life but it was Brackett's, and so he expected nothing as he sat behind the wheel of his car. Two minutes was all he would wait and if Loomis didn't appear by that time, then he would have to take his agony elsewhere. It would be regretted because Brackett was, by nature, a curious man. But he would not persist. The fact that, after having stated this, Brackett remained in the Buick for nine minutes not two is simply because philosophy doesn't always pay the rent. So he waited on the assumption that any man who was scared was a prospective client, especially if he looked as if he could afford to be. Loomis however, despite Brackett's tactics, apparently thought otherwise for he didn't appear.

Brackett sighed (trapeze artist finding himself in the net yet again) and started the engine when the passenger door suddenly opened and a voice said:

'*Walter!* Walter Brackett. Shit, it's been a long time.'

Brackett looked round startled to see the sun-tanned face of a man in his mid-forties grinning at him, one hand on the door, the other on the roof of the car. Tan two-button suit, shantung tie. Tiffany belt buckle – the bronze rectangular kind that were made to advertise anything from Wells Fargo to Barnum & Bailey. This one was a bas-relief of a stockyard with the words *Central & Union Pacific Railroad Co.*

'Don't say you've forgotten me, Walter, after all those steaks we used to share at the Tadich.'

Brackett smiled and nodded. The man was called Herb Johanssen. Father of three, husband of one. Used to be a patrolman ten years ago or more and was liked by almost everyone, including Brackett.

'Of course I do, but I didn't recognize you without your nightstick. Where have you been?'

'You name it, I've been sent there,' Johanssen replied, easing himself on to the edge of the seat. 'They've shuffled me around so often I thought I was a deck of cards.'

'And now you're what? Detective Sergeant?'

'Detective *Lieutenant*,' Johanssen emphasized. 'Homicide.'

Brackett was impressed and said so.

Johanssen smiled. He was not, contrary to his Scandinavian ancestry, tall, blond and sauna-scrubbed. He was, in fact, overweight, almost bald and as intimidating, in appearance, as a curtsey. Promotion, like beauty it seems, is more than skin deep.

'So you're back with us at last,' Brackett said. 'After what – eleven years?'

Johanssen nodded then looked at Brackett.

'So what you doing here, Walter, on a miserable day like this?'

'Identification. Some girl was killed on the bridge.'

'Oh yeh. I heard.'

Silence. Both men stared through the windscreen at the car park. There suddenly seemed nothing more to say.

'Well ...' Brackett said. 'Maybe we could try one of those steaks again later.'

'Sure. But this time, *I'll* pay. Tell me – how's business?'

Brackett tipped the wings of his right hand.

'Still living above Fatty's?' Johanssen asked.

'Cheap rent.'

'What about Kemble? I hear he –'

'He's fine,' Brackett interrupted quickly.

'Good to hear. You know, I never thought anyone could survive a beating like that, but then I never could figure Harry out.'

'Well, Harry's always been tough.'

'Don't I know it. Where is he now?'

'Retired. Unofficially.'

'That's a pity. He was very good. I tell you Walter, if he'd been a cop, I'd *never* make commissioner.'

'Is that what you want?' Brackett asked.

Johanssen smiled, then put his hand on Brackett's shoulder. 'It's good to see you...'

Brackett didn't answer. He glanced back towards the morgue but the door remained defiantly closed. He had lost.

'Still got the same old car,' Johanssen said, patting the dashboard as if it were a neighbour's dog. 'I remember when you first bought this. Shit, I was jealous.'

'I'd better go,' Brackett said and waited as Johanssen moved away, not looking at him. Yes. Still the same old car.

'Don't forget that steak,' Johanssen said, closing the door.

Brackett smiled briefly then drove slowly across the parking lot. When he reached the street, he stopped and looked back through the rear-view mirror to see Johanssen standing watching him. He saw him wave, saw him carefully adjust the flap of one of the pockets of his two-hundred-dollar suit; saw him framed before the backdrop of the red-brick building that harboured his success.

Brackett felt old.

*

He drove back past the marmalade-and-glass skyscrapers of Montgomery (one of them having the audacity to be built like a cap for a dunce), past the banks and the offices, until the street became narrower, faces changed from white to sepia to black to white again, and Brackett entered the parochial familiarity of his own grimy allotment. He made the usual calls, visited the usual bars and asked for his card back from the usual drugstores because he couldn't afford to have them printed any more.

At the corner of Van Buren and Blake (a block that should never have survived the earthquake), Brackett stopped, as he always did, partly out of habit but mostly out of masochism. He stared at the house where his wife had once lived before she had become Mrs Brackett. Her mother still occupied the same two rooms, and for a while after Dorothy had died, Brackett would visit her, walk up the stairs and stay for an hour or so, drinking coffee after the television had been turned down. Not off completely, but just down to simmering, a distraction of panel games in the corner. At first, the two people had avoided talking about Dorothy, shying away from the subject, but then, within a month as photographs were framed and placed on the mantel, they discussed nothing else; the mother recounting memories of the adolescence, while Brackett remembered the marriage, even the pain of those later years long after the orange blossom had faded.

Then, inevitably, the visits stopped as nerve-ends were exposed and Dorothy Mannering competed with Dorothy Brackett, daughter versus wife. And so Brackett left suddenly one day after staying no more than a few minutes, and though it was never stated, the mother knew he would never return. In a way, she was grateful and that was that. Once, when Brackett did come back after an absence of two months, the door wasn't opened to him even though he could hear the television. He knocked loudly four or five times, ignoring the stares of a neighbour's child along the corridor, then turned and walked back down to the street. It was the last time he had ever been in the building.

Brackett reversed the Buick back into the main street. Normally, being a man of routine, he would now drive to Monterey or Carmel, or perhaps to Big Sur. Taking in the fresh air. If it still existed. Instead, the Saturday itinerary had been broken (the image of the wisp of hair reappeared. *Happens all the time*), and so he drove back to his apartment and discovered, within a few minutes, that the file on Mary Malewski was no longer there.

4

At first Brackett believed he had made a mistake. It was possible that he had remembered her name incorrectly (an unlikely occurrence nevertheless), and yet it was no more than three months ago and his filing system was as reliable as the tide.

'Sergeant Henderson? This is Walter Brackett.'

'Who?'

'Brackett. The rich fucking hustler you saw this morning.'

'Oh yeh. What you got?'

'The girl's name *is* Mary Malewski. It's in my appointment book. But no address.'

'I thought you said you had a file on her.'

'I did have. But . . . I lost it.'

'Jesus Christ, what kind of – listen, Brackett, are you sure her name's Malewski?'

'That's the name she gave me. But don't try the directory. I've done it. She's not listed nor known.'

'You're a great help. You know that?'

'Yes. I know it.'

Brackett put the phone down and stared across the desk at the empty chair. He could still remember the girl sitting there wearing a tee-shirt and jeans, sitting nervously and telling him some story about wanting to find her father. Brackett had said he would try and had written down her name and an address in New York where she had once lived. He had begun to ask other questions. *Why did she want to find her father? Why not her mother? How old was she?* But the girl had suddenly become incoherent and said she needed money. Brackett had finally given the girl ten dollars himself, saying that, if she was serious about hiring him, to call him the next day. A cynic might say that the money probably helped to kill her, but Brackett didn't want to think about that. He just knew that Mary Malewski never did call again and that a seemingly meaningless file, two pages no less, was gone. Nothing else. The question, if it mattered, was why – and to Brackett it mattered a great deal. He hated these invisible mosquitoes that irritated his routine; puzzles that didn't quite fit. They disturbed the pattern of his mind, especially if they concerned the dead body of a girl.

'Mr Liebermann!' Brackett shouted from the top of the stairs.

Immediately, the anxious face of the Hungarian appeared below.

'Mr Liebermann – did anyone visit me while I was out? Anyone at all?'

'The police –'

'I know about them. Anyone else?'

'No, Mr Brackett.'

'Are you sure?'

'Well, I was out back some of the time –'

'But no one went into my room?'

Of course, it could have been taken any time in the past three months, but even so, visitors were not exactly waiting in line.

'No, Mr Brackett. Only me.'

Brackett stared at Liebermann.

'*You* went into my room? What for?'

'Well . . . I wanted to leave you the message. The man said it was important.'

'What message?'

'I put it under the ashtray. Just as you and Mr Kemble have always said. Isn't that what –'

But Brackett was already in his room and unfolding the ridiculous piece of paper (greaseproof the size of a chess square) and attempting to read Liebermann's writing. It appeared to state a man's name, a motel and a time. The time was legible and the motel could be guessed at.

'He telephoned ten minutes before you arrived, Mr Brackett.'

The Hungarian was now standing at the door, the look of a penitent on his face.

'What's his name?' Brackett asked. 'Veemey? Veemin?'

'I'm sure I wrote it down correctly, Mr Brackett.'

'You probably did but I can't read it. Look at it.'

Liebermann took the piece of paper and Brackett waited as the

Hungarian searched for a pair of spectacles and slowly fitted them over each ear.

'Well, the motel is called –'

'The man's name. That's all.'

'He said you would know him –'

'His *name*, for Christ's sake.'

'Loomis,' Liebermann replied as if all the world knew. 'Mr Loomis. Would that be right?'

Brackett stared at the paper then turned towards the window.

'Did he say what he wanted?'

'Only that he had to talk to you.'

Mary Malewski. A missing file. And now Loomis. Little pieces of sky. That's all they were. Little jigsaw pieces of sky.

The first sign (yellow and black, the shape of a lozenge) was stuck to the right of the glass in the position of north north-east if one views the window from the street. It read SANDWICHES, and then specified in descending order: *Roast Beef, Corned Beef, Virginia Ham, Turkey, Pastrami*. At each corner, written in emphasis as well as design was the single word HOT encircled in red. Below the sign was a small rectangle stating simply EAT HERE. To the south, and composing the whole of the lower plane of the window, was a row of trays, in varying shades of ochre and saffron, containing fried chicken, stuffed clams, fried fillet and hot buttered corn, ranging in price from 99 cents to $1.69. To the north, a neon, another sign, and then to the west itself, a gummed placard the size of an ottoman announcing HOT BAR-B-Q CHICKEN at $2.19 on a field of scarlet. Below that the words KOSHER & NON-KOSHER, spliced, between the ampersand and the negative, by a pair of eyes.

The eyes are real, though one could be forgiven for thinking otherwise. They don't blink nor move nor indeed show any emotion whatsoever. They merely stare through the glass, through the letters and across the street. As if, to the casual observer, they are merely passing the time of the day.

Brackett finished his lunch (a potato salad prepared by Mrs Liebermann) and considered the day. It was one forty-eight and the appointment was at two thirty.

'Is that the Park 'n Rest motel?' he asked, holding the receiver in one hand as he attempted to fill a cup of Southern Comfort with the other.

'Yes, sir,' came the reply. 'Can I help you?'

'Are you the only Park 'n Rest in the Bay Area?'

'Yes, şir.'

'But you have other branches?'

'In every state, sir. Every star on our nation's flag is a Park 'n Rest.'

'But you're the only one in Sausalito?'

'Indeed, sir.'

'Then do you have a Mr Loomis staying with you?'

'Well, it's not really our policy –'

'It's not? Fine. I'll tell Governor Reagan that.'

A long pause, then the voice returned. Diminutive seventh.

'Who did you say was calling, sir?'

'I didn't. Just tell me about Mr Loomis.'

'Well. . . One moment, sir.'

Brackett sipped at the drink. He hated to admit it, but good American whiskey, with an 'e', really was superior to Scotch. Especially neat.

'Would that be Mr J. Loomis?'

'How many Loomis's are there?'

'Just the one.'

'What room?'

'Forty-one. Shall I put you –'

'No, I'll break the news personally. Thank you.'

'You're welc –'

Brackett put down the phone and wrote 'Loomis J.' on a blank piece of paper, then sat at the desk for perhaps ten minutes recalling all the conversation that had taken place at the morgue. Most of that he wrote down as well. It seemed important – not to him, but to Loomis. And yet if he wanted to talk, why did he refuse the ride earlier?

Brackett stood up and his gaze rested on the photograph of Dorothy. He looked at the face of his wife and read the inscription as if it were the first time. He was pleased she had liked the present.

'How did you guess that's exactly what I always wanted?'

'Well, I'm a detective, aren't I?'

Yes he was. And he had been for twenty-five years since the day he met Kemble. He had accepted the job at first with naive romanticism, as if they were Spade and Marlowe and the world was filled with fat men and little sisters waiting to hire them. They believed in their dreams as the cards were printed and their names were painted on the office door, until all too soon they realized that they hadn't just stepped out of the pages of *Dime Detective*. That was simply what they were worth.

When success did come and the dime became a grand, they thought the partnership would never end; but it did end, abruptly in one single night as they picked the shell of Kemble out of the gutter and Brackett was on his own. He continued of course, for the telephone still rang. His spirit, however, was broken and he knew it, though he would never admit it. He blundered on in his part long after the curtain had come down and the audience had left. An ageing bit-player refusing to leave the stage and too stubborn to accept that only the props remained.

'Mr Brackett?'

And yet Brackett *was* still a detective, even if his name was in small print. He even had a genuine client now. With Loomis, he was back in business.

'Mr Brackett?'

He might even buy a new car. A Jaguar or a Citroën. Nothing too fancy.

'Mr Brackett – I did knock twice.'

The woman was standing in the centre of the room.

'It's about my dog. I was ... hoping that you might have found him.'

Brackett turned slowly as the woman gazed up at him as if the lost dog meant everything in the world to her.

'I thought ... that you might have some news.'

'I'm sorry, Mrs Markstein,' Brackett said. 'I haven't seen him.'

The woman looked at the leash she was clutching in her hand, then reluctantly walked back to the door.

'Do you think he's lost for ever, Mr Brackett?'

There was no answer. The door was closed and Brackett stood

listening to the footsteps as they descended slowly to the delicatessen below.

The car hesitated at the top of the ramp like a diver assessing the depth of the water below, then slowly moved down into the semi-darkness of the basement. A black garage-hand leaning against a metal railing raised his head then waved the vehicle on, gesturing towards the painted arrows on the concrete floor.

The driver kept the windows shut, as he had been told, driving slowly until he reached the circular revolve. Then almost immediately he heard the whine of machinery, cog-wheels connecting, and the car swivelled round till it was facing the avenue of brushes and leather and streams of water. Tyres slotted into metal rails and the car lurched forward and soap poured over the windscreen, transforming the glass into a nimbus sky. Music was heard from the speakers as the passenger emerged from the floor and locked the radio dial on to a record of Big Band jazz (*Sing Sing Sing*. Harry James on trumpet), and then the car was moving through a curtain, then another and the driver could see the giant roller-brushes descend, creep along the bonnet and over the roof like midnight creatures attracted by the light. A third curtain and the water descended, the orchestra moved into a riff, an audience applauded and the driver began to panic as suddenly the passenger pulled on the handbrake, set the car in reverse and the wheels began to jam. They jammed, locked, and the car keeled over to the side in an explosion of water and shattered glass. The driver turned as a piano played, turned as a loose roller smashed against the nearside wing, turned towards the passenger as soap eased through the hinges of the doors and into the grille and over his shoes, and then he opened his mouth to scream and a voice said:

'Keep it open, Baby, and suck on this.'

5

Brackett drove fast towards Sausalito, hesitating only as he crossed the Golden Gate Bridge out of curiosity to see where the accident had happened; but the traffic was too fast, as lunch-time tourists hurried to Muir Woods to gawp at the redwoods. At the toll, Brackett turned right, moving down along the west of the Bay, past the main promenade of Sausalito itself (Trident Restaurant on the right) until finally he saw the neon sign, the coy admission that there were still vacancies, and stopped outside the Park 'n Rest.

It was like any other motel and that, at least, to Brackett, was predictable. To him, the hamburger, baseball, Coca-Cola, what-you-will, were never the true symbol of America, despite the propaganda. It was the motel, plain and simple, where the founding fathers (adopting pen names) had etched the image of the nation. The Park 'n Rest, aware that it was in Sausalito and not downtown Detroit, had attempted to display a little class. A mock courtyard, plus fountain, had been built as a form of atrium, fringed by the various rooms, but otherwise it wouldn't have fooled a bat. Brackett ignored the decor and walked past the office to Room 41. It was on the first floor in a far corner and as silent as an urn.

Brackett knocked twice, then opened the door, surprised to find it unlocked. The room was empty. That was obvious immediately, as was the chair upturned on the floor, the broken lamp, a suitcase scattering its contents into a corner. A telephone off the hook. It was also obvious that a struggle had taken place, though one that was short-lived. There was no blood, no signs of serious violence; merely an indication that an intruder had surprised Loomis, and, after the requisite resistance, had ordered him out of the room, probably with a gun, closed the door and taken him away.

Brackett swore out of anger, cursing himself as he realized that all this had probably happened while he was drinking his second bourbon or admiring the view from the bay. His only consolation was that it wasn't entirely his fault, since he had arrived on time. In fact, five minutes early, but that was a pathetic excuse. He should have known. He had seen Loomis's face, the terror, and he should have known what might happen. The knife turned as he admitted that ten years ago, five even, he *would* have done.

The hairshirt however could wait for another day, for perhaps there was still time. He glanced through the suitcase, found nothing, opened the door into the bathroom and saw nothing there either except the sink, two towels, an aerosol can of shaving foam, a box of Kleenex, and a woman crouched shivering and naked on the floor staring at him as if petrified with fear. Which she was. Brackett closed the door and looked down at her.

'It's all right ...' he began inadequately. 'I won't hurt you. I'm a friend of Loomis.'

The woman didn't move, clutching her knees with her hands. She was dark-haired, overweight and plain, her face embellished only by a bruise below the left eye.

'Look, there's no one else here,' Brackett said, opening the door wide and gesturing into the other room. He then went to the bed, found a dress and some underclothes tangled among the blankets and returned to the bathroom. The woman hadn't moved.

'Here you are. You'll catch cold.'

The woman stared at the clothes as they were dropped by her feet and Brackett turned discreetly away to allow her to dress, when suddenly she was standing up and running towards him, screaming and hammering her fists against him. Brackett seized her wrist and slapped her and pushed her against the wall, then slapped her again as she tried to bite him.

'Listen to me – I don't want to hurt you –' he shouted, then pulled her up off the floor as the tears came and the woman slumped down on to the lid of the toilet seat, holding him for support. Brackett put one arm around her waist, steadying her, and reached out for the bath towel to cover her shoulders.

'My name's Walter Brackett,' he said, kneeling down in front of her. 'I came here to see Loomis. He was here, wasn't he?'

There was a pause, then the woman nodded.

'Good,' Brackett said. 'Now what happened,'

Silence. He could see freckles of needle marks on the woman's arms which she quickly covered with the towel.

'It's all right. I'm not from the police,' Brackett said, reading her thoughts. 'I just want to find your friend.'

Slowly the woman raised her head (denim blue eyes, neck like guy-ropes) and looked at Brackett for a long time, then said finally:

'He's going to kill him.'

'Who?'

'He made me ... stay here and said that if I moved he'd –'

'Look he's gone. See? No one. You're all right.'

The partition door was opened wide in emphasis.

'Who was he?' Brackett asked.

The woman swivelled her head round, then the jaw was raised eliminating the upper lip, a caricature of defiance. Brackett had seen it all before.

'All right,' he said patiently. 'Just tell me what he looked like. His appearance. Old? Young?'

'Black.'

Brackett stared at her:

'Black? He was black?'

A shrug.

'You said he was black,' Brackett insisted. 'Do you mean his skin? What?'

The woman hesitated:

'Black...'

'You don't seem very sure.'

'Black.' More emphatic. 'Aren't they all black?'

'Aren't *who* all black?'

Silence. Brackett sighed, then lit a cigarette for something to do, throwing the match into the sink.

'Am *I* black?' he asked casually. 'Would you say *I* was?'

Another shrug. The scene now reminded Brackett of those childhood charades when the scion of the family (invariably christened *What's the matter darling?*) doesn't want to play the game any more.

'Look,' Brackett said. 'I've got to find him whatever he is. Just stay here and you'll be all right. Lock the door.'

He picked up her clothes and placed them on her lap, adding:

'Do you know where they went?'

'No...'

'You didn't hear them say anything?'

'No.'

'Thanks a lot,' Brackett said and walked to the door.

'By the way, what's your name?'

'Norma Wheatley.'

'How well did you know Loomis, Norma?'

No answer. Not that it was needed.

'All right. Just tell me – you don't know a girl called Mary Malewski, do you?'

The woman shook her head then began to shiver again. Brackett stopped and studied her and the whole pitiful vulgarity of it all. *I tell you, Walter, we'll have our business cards embossed. Embossed in italics. Got to impress the clients.*

'I'm sorry I hurt you,' Brackett said, then left as the woman began to vomit, head between knees, on to the neat pink-and-blue tiled floor.

The old man at the desk asked him if he was a cop and Brackett said he wasn't but he would still like to know the answer to his question and that twenty dollars was all he could spare.

'A blue Plymouth.'

'And that was Loomis's own car?'

'Well, he arrived in it.'

'Was he driving or was it the other man?'

'Who said there was another man?'

'Didn't you see anyone else?'

'I just saw Loomis. I didn't take much notice.'

'Well, you don't happen to know which way he went, do you?'

'Where he went?'

'Yes. Right? Left?'

'Neither, mister. He went straight across the street.'

Brackett stared puzzled through the office window.

'To where?'

'What do you mean – to where? To the car-wash. What else is there across the street?'

But even as Brackett was running, he knew it was too late. He could see the people at the top of the ramp, and as he pushed through, ignoring the shouts, he could see the blue Plymouth and he knew that Loomis was inside it. The wreckage of machinery, the radio still tuned, and the shattered glass. And beneath the car, the slow ebbing of soap and foam that was now the colour of a flamingo.

'Who's dead?' a woman asked and Brackett heard someone reply that he didn't know as he walked to the metal railing, his back to the Plymouth. A garage-hand walked towards him, offered him a cigarette and said:

'Jesus what a mess. You see it?'

Brackett stared at the faces at the entrance to the basement, then asked:

'What colour is he?'

'What colour?'

'I mean is he white or black?'

'White. What's left of him. What kind of fucking question is that?'

'See anyone else in the car when it arrived?'

'No. Why? You a cop?'

'No.'

'Didn't even see the car. Who looks at cars?'

Someone else asked if the police had been called but there was no need for a reply, for already Brackett could hear the electronic banshee of police cars as they approached from the south.

'Any place near here,' he said, 'I can get a drink?'

When Brackett returned an hour later, the basement of the garage was producing irritation. It was hot and the ventilation system was almost nil. There were probably thirty people around the car-wash itself, including detectives, stenographers, photographers, officials from the police laboratory, a medical examiner, three patrolmen, a representative from the District Attorney, garage-hands, onlookers and the corpse of Loomis lying on the front seat of the Plymouth with powder-burns surrounding what was left of his mouth.

Near the office, the owner was attempting to seek recompense for the damaged machinery of his *Magic Auto Wash* and being told to put it in writing. Politeness was for the few. In a far corner, sitting on the only chair, a tall, thin man (Simmons) watched everything with obvious frustration, which was forgivable.

Conversations to be recorded, but not in any particular sequence. No waiter leading us (tray of drinks in hand) from one guest to another. Just questions and answers and nothing more.

Pedantic:

'What time did he arrive?'

'I told you. I didn't see him arrive.'

'Did you see the car arrive?'

'Yes. I saw the car arrive.'

'So what time did the *car* arrive?'

'Two o'clock. Two fifteen.'

'Which one?'

'Two o'clock.'

'Why not two fifteen?'

'All right. Two fifteen.'

'Don't agree with me. What time?'

'Two five.'

Casual:

'You must have been very busy. I appreciate that. But isn't it usual for a customer to buy a ticket first?'

'Yes, but –'

'Then why didn't he?'

'Well, I . . .'

'Miss –?'

'Della Fici.'

'Miss Della Fici. Pretty name. Why didn't you notice?'

'We weren't busy. Not really.'

'So what were you doing?'

'I was . . .'

'You were in there?'
'Well – I didn't realize.'
'Can't you hear a car engine from in there?'
'Not really.'
'Don't be embarrassed, Miss Della Fici. It's a natural bodily function.'
Academic:
'Charlie – do you want some pictures of the back seat?'
'Why? What's on the back seat?'
'The other half of his head.'
Questions. Simmons sighed and stared at Brackett, then walked across the basement stepping carefully over puddles of soap, till he reached him.
'Excuse me – but do you know Loomis? The dead man?'
Brackett turned, surprised.
'I'm just asking,' Simmons continued, a slight smile, 'because you don't look like . . . a passer-by.'
'We met this morning.'
'Is that a fact? And where was that?'
'At the morgue.'
Simmons raised his eyebrows, smiled again, then glanced at a notebook.
'Well, that makes you either Sergeant John Henderson or Walter Brackett. And you're not Sergeant Henderson because he's fatter than you and I've just been talking to him for the last half hour. So Walter Brackett, right?'
'Yes.'
'Fine. Come and sit down, Brackett. My name's Lieutenant Simmons. And there's my badge.'
Brackett made no comment but studied the detective, noticing the vanity in the polished shoes and the lacquered hair. They sat on a low shelf above drums of oil. Questions.
'So what brings you here, Brackett. Ghoulish curiosity?'
'Is that what you think? '
'If I did, you'd be on the other side of the barriers just like those creatures over there. So why are you here?'
'Loomis called me.'
'Did he now? And what did he want?'
'I don't know. He was dead when I arrived.'

'Is that a fact?'

Brackett glanced at Simmons, who leant back, careful not to let his suit touch the garage wall.

'Am I under suspicion?' Brackett asked.

'But of course you are, Brackett.'

There was a beat and Simmons smiled, a mere split-second widening of the mouth, then added:

'Just like two hundred million others at the moment. When we don't know who's guilty, *everyone's* guilty, wouldn't you say?'

'No,' Brackett said.

Simmons glanced at him. Nearby Johanssen was talking to a reporter.

'Oh, of course, I forgot. You're a private whatever, aren't you?'

'I'd still disagree with you.'

'Nevertheless, Brackett, you are. So why don't you narrow the number down for me.'

'From two hundred million?'

'From two hundred million.'

Brackett hesitated.

'Don't be shy, Brackett,' Simmons said. 'I'm humble enough to listen to . . . experience.'

It wasn't a compliment and Brackett knew it.

'Well, first. Unless the murderer's got a private jet, he's still in the area. That cuts out the millions. Secondly, he's a man. That cuts out the thousands. Thirdly, he's black. That cuts out the hundreds. Fourthly, he's a professional killer not an amateur, and that cuts out the tens. And *fifthly*, since he's a professional, he's almost certainly got a record for something or other. Which means you have his prints on file somewhere. Which also means that if you dust everything from the Plymouth to Room 41 of the Park 'n Rest motel, you'll find a set that matches. Which cuts out the units, leaving you, not with two hundred million, but just one single one. Anything else?'

Simmons raised his head slowly and looked at Brackett and suddenly smiled.

'Well, well – so it's as simple as that?'

'No. But you asked a question and I answered it.'

'You certainly did. Tell me, where were you standing when you saw the murder?'

'I didn't see it.'

'Oh? Then you obviously saw the murderer?'

'No.'

'Then I should hand in my badge, Brackett, because I'm just in the dark and I hate the fact that the dear citizens of San Francisco are paying their taxes to support an incompetent like me. It almost amounts to extortion.'

Brackett sighed:

'There's a woman in Room 41. Her name's Norma Wheatley. *She* saw the killer.'

'There was no one in Room 41 when we arrived.'

'She was there an hour ago.'

'Well, she's not there now.'

'All right, she's not there now. But I've told you her name. All you have to do is find her –'

'That's all?'

Brackett turned angrily towards Simmons:

'Now, listen –'

'No. *You* listen, Brackett,' Simmons said, his voice low. 'See that man over there?'

A beat, then Brackett stared across the basement.

'Which one?' he asked, reclaiming his temper.

Simmons gestured towards a small, thin man standing by one of the concrete pillars, standing alone and watching the proceedings around him with an expression of increasing disillusion like air escaping from a tired balloon. Other than that, he was as conspicuous as a kerb stone.

'What about him?' Brackett said.

'Just be thankful you're not talking to *him*.'

'Why? Who is he?'

'He works for the B. N. Double-Dee, that's who.'

'A narc?'

'Clever boy,' Simmons said as if talking to a dog that had just learnt to sit. 'A narc.'

He didn't elaborate, even if he needed to. Brackett understood completely, or at least appreciated the reason why Loomis's death had suddenly brought out the police hierarchy. For even though he himself had never been directly concerned with drug traffic (its chic image had snubbed his generation), he had seen the films and read the books like everyone else. Loomis, he was to learn later, had been a mule, a courier, someone who had to be kept alive until it was discovered who was paying for his stamps. Now that he was dead, it was the old etcetera, and Brackett accepted it merely as landscape. To him, a prospective client had been killed. That's what mattered. The puzzle, Harry. The evergreen seek-and-find.

'Brackett, in a way I agree with you.'

Simmons was now talking, the Bureau Agent dismissed like a scene-shifter between acts.

'What?' Brackett said, focusing back. To his right, Johanssen was now posing for a photographer from the *Chronicle.*

'I said I agree with you. A little.'

Simmons smiled, a strobe smile, and ran his index finger along the length of one eyebrow.

'I agree,' he continued, 'that whoever killed Loomis behaved like a professional, but whether he's hired or self-employed is another matter. The odds are, however, he knew Loomis to get that close. But he's no amateur. An amateur wouldn't have the confidence to go all through this and get away with it. He wouldn't take the risk. He'd shoot Cock Robin right in that motel room and we'd have him before he hit the kerb. But this boy has no fear about killing. He gets a kick out of the danger, and an amateur doesn't put a gun in his victim's mouth unless he's sick. So one point to you, Brackett. But you really mustn't go around blaming everything on the poor little niggers. It gives the police a bad name –'

'She said he was black.'

'Who said?'

'The woman in the motel.'

'*If* she exists.'

'She does exist. I saw her.'

'But no one else did.'

'It's a *motel*, lieutenant, not a checking-in lounge –'

'I'm aware of that. I'm a big boy. But the fact is – and we're talking about *facts* – no one else saw her but you.'

'And Loomis –'

'He's dead.'

'And the man who killed him. He saw her and if you don't get to Norma Wheatley first, *she'll* be dead too.'

A silence. Brackett became aware of faces staring at him. Beside him, Simmons carefully recrossed his legs, inhaled at a cigarette, then said finally:

'All right, Brackett. Let's say she does exist.'

'She does.'

'But how can you be sure she wasn't lying?'

'Why should she?'

'Why *should* she? Because there's a lot of people in this damn country who'd be quite happy to burn every black that ever was born. That's why.'

'She had no cause –'

'Who the hell is talking about *causes*! Now you just tell me this – do you *really* think she was telling the truth?'

Brackett hesitated, then shook his head. He had to admit it. No.

'I don't think she knew *what* she was saying,' he said. 'No, I don't think she was telling the truth.'

Brackett looked away, wanting to leave but feeling obliged to stay for reasons he couldn't explain. He felt nervous, out of condition, or more accurately – though he would be reluctant to admit it – out of his depth.

'Brackett ...' Simmons said after a moment, keeping in profile. 'Let's say Norma Wheatley was right. Let's assume that everything you said was true. *You* weren't lying and *she* wasn't lying. Now, I asked you a question a while back and you answered it. *I'm* going to answer it now.'

Brackett stared at Simmons warily.

'What proof have we,' Simmons continued in a voice usually reserved for instructors of the retarded. 'What proof have we that the same man who went into that motel room was also in the Plymouth? No one, including the old man at the motel, saw anyone in the car except Loomis.'

'So he was hiding on the floor.'

'But was it the same man? Have you the *proof*?'

'Of course not. All I can say is that it was probable.'

'Exactly. Probable and no more, and that wouldn't get us to

first base. So we're back in the hundreds. Not even in the tens, but the hundreds. And then, if he's a professional – and we both agree he probably is – he's not going to leave his prints on anything. Not on that Plymouth, not in that motel room. Nowhere. That boy's so clever he'll even wipe his cock clean before he comes out of the john. Which puts us back in the thousands again, doesn't it? And then, God help us, if he's evaded everything we've put up against him and he's on a T.W.A. jet looking over the Sierras at this very moment, then ... it's the millions again.'

A pause and Simmons added quietly:

'Not quite so cut and dried after all. Is it, Brackett?'

The man, standing at the rail of the *Harbor Queen* ferry, stared at the receding houses of Sausalito and waited till the boat was in the centre of the Bay. After confirming that he was alone, he took the gun, hidden in a sock, from his inside pocket, leant over the rail and opened his hands. He watched the heavy woollen bundle fall, hit the surface of the water and disappear. Then he walked back to his table under the glass roof, finished his beer and ordered another. A Tuborg. Just the bottle, Baby.

Brackett stood by the open doors of the Plymouth. He had glimpsed the body of Loomis for a brief moment and that was enough. Death was a hideous aberration to anyone's life, even if it was encountered while nestled against pillows, grandchildren hemming the counterpane, or on the battlefield beneath the banners of one's country. It was neither blessed nor heroic nor any of those cosy adjectives that the pious living declaimed in pulpit or sonnet or in the tardy eulogies of the obituary. Death *was* just the end of a life, and if Loomis (and it had now been officially confirmed that it was him) believed that the act of a muzzle of a ·38 being placed in his mouth and spattering his brains on to the beige vinyl of a Plymouth sedan was simply *playing hookey*, then heaven help him because Brackett couldn't any more.

'Mourn him, Brackett, because no one else will. When the State gives him a coffin, he'll probably steal the handles.'

Brackett made no comment but watched the soap and water, white and carnadine, being hosed into a drain.

'We've put out an A.P.B. on Norma Wheatley,' Simmons continued. 'We'll find her. Junkies are the easy ones.'

Brackett turned and began to walk away when Simmons side-stepped in front of him.

'Keep out of this,' he said, in a manner that needed little elaboration. 'This is our case.'

'So?' Brackett asked. 'What would you do? Take away my licence? You can't touch me, lieutenant, unless I do something illegal.'

'The statute books are very big, Brackett. You'd be surprised what you can find in them.'

'I know. I've read them.'

He continued walking but Simmons moved emphatically in front of him again:

'Brackett – what's Loomis to you?'

'Nothing. I only met him this morning.'

'Coincidence.'

'You could say that.'

Simmons smiled and said:

'Oh ... tell me, do you ever get homesick to go back to England?'

'Now and then.'

'Don't get homesick without letting us know, will you?'

Simmons gave a cold camera-shutter wink and walked away, merging into the crowd until he was lost from sight. Brackett didn't move for a moment until he suddenly became aware of the voices and the smoke, people jostling past him, and hurried towards the exit and the coolness of the street air. As he reached the ramp, he heard a voice call out his name. Brackett ignored it and tried to push through the barriers but Johanssen had reached him.

'Walter! Don't rush away.'

'Call me sometime, Herb. I'm in a hurry.'

'But I wanted to invite you to our house for dinner. My wife would love to see you.'

Brackett stopped and looked at Johanssen.

'I'm sorry, Herb. I didn't mean to . . . Another time. All right? And give my best to Hilary.'

'*Hilary?*' Johanssen said, startled.

'Isn't your wife called Hilary?'

'No. Virginia. Hilary and I got divorced four years ago.'

'Oh. Then give my best to Virginia.'

Brackett smiled and made his way towards the street. As he reached the Buick, Johanssen caught up with him, his face anxious.

'Walter – are you all right?'

'I'm fine. . .'

'If it's anything to do with Simmons, don't let him worry you. You should hear how he talks to me.'

'You're going to get run over, Herb.'

Johanssen glanced startled around him and stepped quickly on to the sidewalk.

'Any plans, Walter?' he asked as he assumed his adopted pose of authority once more, the one he was rehearsing for the cover of *Time*.

Brackett studied the entrance to the auto-wash, then the motel and said:

'There's a job I turned down a couple of months ago. I've just decided to accept it.'

'Oh well, that's fine, Walter.'

Brackett opened the car door, noticed Johanssen's expression and added:

'It's all right. I won't be following you and Simmons. It's just that a girl once asked me to find her father. I've decided to do just that.'

'Oh,' Johanssen said, visibly relieved. 'Well, if there's anything I can do. Anything at all. I remember how you helped me in the old days –'

'Herb, there *is* something.'

'Just name it, Walter.'

'Do you remember that girl who was killed in the crash last night?'

Johanssen hesitated.

'Well . . . I wasn't there, Walter.'

'I know. But where would her car be taken?'

'It depends. If we were checking it out or it's stolen or whatever, it'd probably be at the yard on the corner of Battery and Lingfield.'

'That's near the docks, isn't it?'

'Yeh. Near there. But you'd need a pass.'

'Sure. Couldn't you fix it?'

This time, Johanssen almost shuffled his feet.

'Well ... I'd like to ... Walter. But it's not really...'

'That's all right, Herb,' Brackett said.

'Don't want to blot my copybook. Know what I mean?'

'I understand, Herb.'

'I mean, anything else –'

'I said I understand, Herb. Give my best to Virginia. All right?'

Johanssen nodded. Brackett smiled, patted him on the shoulder, then said:

'A phone? Is there one near here?'

'In the garage.'

'I'd rather not go in there again.'

'Well, there's one in the Deli.'

He pointed to a delicatessen next to the motel.

'Thanks, Herb,' Brackett said, patted the shoulder once more, and walked away. Johanssen watched him until he had entered the delicatessen, then adjusted his tie and returned to the auto-wash and the reporters.

The delicatessen was almost as crowded as the garage basement, though nobody seemed to be buying, despite the array of stickers on the window. Most of the people were congregated around the counter discussing the drama across the street and wondering what the world was coming to. Brackett had to shout to ask where the phone was and if he could use it, and a voice from the midst said it was in the corner and help yourself.

'Thanks,' Brackett said as he paused to admire the shop that Liebermann would envy, and then picked up the phone and dialled. A woman's voice answered, cautious and slightly out of breath.

'Hallo?'

'Miriam?' Brackett said. 'Walter Brackett.'

'Walter! How *are* you?'

'Fine. Kids?'

'Fine. When we going to see you?'

'Soon. Soon. Sidney there?'

'Sidney? No, he's out.'

'Is he on duty today?'

'No. Last night. Today he's just out.'

'So when do you expect him back?'

'He said soon. But that was three hours ago.'

'But you do expect him back?'

'Anytime. *You* know Sidney.'

'Well, when he comes in, could you ask him to meet me at the pound on Lingfield and Battery at, say, six o'clock?'

'Where?'

'The pound, Miriam. Lingfield and Battery. Could you do that? It's important.'

'Certainly, Walter. But –'

'Six o'clock, Miriam. See you soon.'

Brackett put down the phone and stared into space. He felt numb and yet strangely excited as he suddenly realized what he was doing. He didn't know what he was looking for exactly, nor even if he'd find anything. He just knew he'd taken the first step. And the direction he wanted to go.

'Thanks,' he said to a man behind the counter handing him a dime. 'For the phone.'

'You a detective too?'

'In a way,' Brackett said.

'He used to come in this shop.'

'Who?'

'The guy who was killed. From the motel. Right?'

Brackett looked at him and then asked:

'Was he alone? When he came in?'

'Always. *All*-ways. Two cartons of Bordens, a jar of Maxwell, Cokes up to here and a hot beef on rye. Sometimes pastrami, but usually the beef.'

'Did he ever talk about anything?'

'Never. Which was a blessing.'

Brackett nodded at the rows of sandwiches.

'And you never saw anyone with him?' he asked.

'No one. Never. I told your buddies.'

'Thanks,' Brackett said and began to push his way from the counter, then turned, a sudden thought, and said:

'He didn't happen to be in here this morning, did he?'

The man studied the ceiling in a reflex action, head on an angle, then replied:

'No. Everyone in the world, yes, but not him. Sorry.'

'It doesn't matter,' Brackett said with a shrug. 'It's not my case.'

He then walked out into the street and stood by the window for a moment, glancing abstractedly at the posters, the lists of sandwiches, and the reflection of the motel opposite. The police barriers were everywhere.

Brackett shivered, returned to the Buick, started the engine and drove away from the kerb. As he circled the car round to the opposite lane, he saw once again the revolving lights, the ambulance, the police cars, and realized that it was still only four twenty-three in the afternoon. And sunny.

There wasn't even the dignity of darkness.

6

It was a Toyota. To be precise, it was a Toyota Crown Custom Estate, mustard in colour, and now lying like a trodden insect in the corner of the pound.

Brackett walked around the car once (a distance of forty feet in the showroom. Here, a mere thirty), replaced the radio aerial into its rear pocket, and realized all too clearly that his speculations (credible as they may have seemed on paper) were wrong. He had thought perhaps that Loomis had not been a pedestrian at all, but a passenger, and he had written that down. He had also written down the alternative that he might have been the driver. That Loomis had sat next to the girl, that they knew each other and that he had lied because of, oh, a million things. He had panicked; he had feared an accusation of manslaughter. Anything.

But Brackett was wrong and he had no defence. Walking around the car again, it was as obvious as the day that if Loomis had been a passenger, he wouldn't have left the car alive, because the door would have trapped him, snared him like a clam, crushed him, and he would have been found, still sitting in the seat, stereo speaker in his lap, and that would be the end of it.

On the other hand, if he *had* been the driver and had sat behind the wheel, he would have gone through the windscreen when the crash occurred, but that privilege had been reserved solely, as evidence showed, for a fourteen-year-old girl (*fourteen* according to the brief note in Brackett's diary) called Mary Malewski. The inevitable conclusion therefore was that she had been on her own, had driven the car on her own and had died on her own, and Loomis had been merely the witness he had claimed to be. It was regrettable but it was so, for if only Brackett could have found a connection right there, in the wreck of a six-cylinder vehicle, he might have unearthed *one* common denominator between them apart from mere coincidence.

Dispirited but still stoically optimistic, he walked back across the gravel towards Assistant Inspector Sidney Horowitz, a friend since the days of Eisenhower, who tolerated his demands (the pass to the pound being one of them) more, Brackett suspected, out of sympathy than anything else. He hadn't exactly been Best Man at Brackett's wedding, but he *had* been a contender.

'Sidney, when did you say the car was stolen?' Brackett asked, studying the undamaged rear of the Toyota and the California plates.

'Last night.'

'The owner said last night?'

'Yes. Last night.'

'And he identified the car?'

'Yes.'

'Did he come here personally, or did you describe it over the phone?'

'We called him. Why see him?'

'And he didn't know who had stolen it?'

'No.'

Horowitz was now beginning to be irritable. He had a cold, he had missed his lunch and he preferred to ask questions, not answer them, especially to someone like Brackett, whom he had once described as looking like a condemned tenement. Why, Brackett had said, he had to suffer these insults from friends he would never know, but he had to admit he liked the imagery.

And the pound itself was, after all, a rather incongruous scene. A surrealistic angel cake of chrome and colour as cars were piled upon trucks upon cars; an avenue of diseased elms to the left descending towards the docks, an oyster sky, the tip of the Coit Tower, and before it all, the two men themselves. One of them (thin, balding) pacing up and down, each step edging nearer to the black-and-white car waiting by the gates; the other, in a suit that was designed twenty years ago, not moving but raising and lowering his voice, a crescendo of questions, in direct relation to the distance of the listener, the shouts of children playing in a vacant lot and the sound of a freighter in the water below.

'Did he report that the car was stolen?' Brackett called out as Horowitz sentried back again towards the gates.

'Who?'

'The owner. Did he report his missing car? Last night, say?'

'Well, no.'

'What?'

'I said no.'

'You mean he didn't know his car was stolen until you told him?'

'Yes.'

'Isn't that unusual? I mean – not to report it?'

'Not really. He might not have needed the car.'

'But look at it. How could he miss it? It's the colour of a canary and the size of a Sherman tank.'

'Walter – what do you expect me to do? Maybe he didn't look out of the window of his house.'

Plausible but nothing more.

'What's his name?' Brackett said.

'Who?'

'Sidney, will you stop walking up and down and listen. I want to know his name.'

Horowitz hesitated, his mouth tightening, and the familiar expression of wariness appeared. It didn't indicate a refusal to answer but simply a legitimate reluctance. Brackett waited as Horowitz glanced back towards his car and the digital pit-a-pat that constituted police chatter, then he finally said:

'Plomer.'

'That's his name or his job?'

'Name. Robert Plomer. P-l-o –'

'Write it down. Next to his address.'

'Now, Walter –'

'I could always look it up in the book, Sidney.'

A pause.

'He lives on Pacific Avenue,' Horowitz said, writing down the address.

'Impressive,' Brackett replied. And it was.

'Is that all, Walter? Because any moment someone's going to ask where I am and I don't want it to be Simmons.'

'One more thing. Did this Plomer know about the girl? I mean, did you mention it?'

'We had to. He might have known who she was.'

'And did he?'

'What?'

'Know who she was?'

'He said no.'

'Sidney, what do you mean – he *said* no.'

'*No*. N.O. He said no. He didn't know a girl called Mary Malewski. And for what it's worth, I believed him.'

Brackett stared at Horowitz then placed the piece of paper in his wallet.

'Thanks.'

Horowitz shrugged:

'What I don't understand, Walter, is – what's in it for you?'

Brackett clicked his tongue.

'Sidney – do I ever ask *you* what your reasons are?'

'No, but –'

'Sidney, let's just say I don't like loose ends.'

'You know that I'm responsible to Simmons.'

'I know,' Brackett said. 'And I thank you.'

'So – oh, fuck it, Walter. You're impossible.'

'Well, as they say, Sidney, the impossible takes a little longer. And I've got all the time in the world.'

Horowitz smiled, then grinned, then finally laughed and hugged Brackett:

'Shit, you'll never change.'

'No,' Brackett said. 'Not even my suit.'

Horowitz moved away and stared at Brackett and shook his head in a mixture of bafflement and affection.

'Well, I wish you luck. But I can tell you now, there's a lot of Malewskis in this country. Especially in New York.'

'But no missing daughter?' Brackett asked.

'Oh sure,' Horowitz said, raising his eyes to heaven. 'One. And she's anywhere between the ages of forty-five and sixty. She's called Ruth and was last seen sitting in a Greyhound bus heading for Grossinger's.'

'Where's Grossinger's?'

'In the Catskills, you schmuck. Where've you been?'

Brackett waggled his hands in mock derision.

'And that's all? No other Malewskis?'

'None, Walter.'

'Doesn't *anyone* report anything missing around here? A car's one thing, but a fourteen-year-old daughter is another.'

'Walter,' Horowitz said with paternal patience. 'When was the last time you were in Missing Persons?'

'Don't ask.'

'Visit it next week. Just go and see it because you won't believe it. People today lose children like cuff-links. Six, seven, eight years old some of them. Go and see it.'

'I believe you, Sidney.'

Horowitz gave a bleak smile, shrugged despairingly, then stared at the Toyota for a long time. Brackett watched his face and knew what he was thinking.

'Poor stupid kid,' Horowitz said and returned to his car. Brackett heard it start, reverse and drive away, saw the brake lights blink at the corner of the block and then it was gone.

Slowly Brackett walked back to the Toyota and ran his hand along the side-windows, picking at the stubbles of glass embedded in the chrome strip, and then almost unconsciously turned the handle of the door that the girl had touched, and opened the door that the girl had opened, as if in some idiotic way he could recreate an answer. The door offered no resistance as the lock released, the handle was pulled and immediately Brackett heard a scream.

There was no mistake about it. A scream splintering the air, a single high-pitched decibel coming from within the car defying him to enter. Startled, Brackett released the door and it fell shut and there was silence. The echo lingered in the air, jarring his nerves, but the scream itself was gone.

Brackett stared at the door, then cautiously repeated the action. The door opened once more to reveal the empty seats, the shriek returned, not human any more but more electronic, and a voice said:

'It's the alarm.'

Brackett spun round and found himself face to face with a

boy in his mid-teens, dressed in green grease-stained overalls, and leaning, grinning at him, on the rear wing of the car.

'What did you say?' Brackett asked, trying hurriedly to stabilize his outer reactions.

'I said it's the alarm. Scares you, don't it?'

'A little.'

The boy grinned again. Brackett realized he wasn't fooling anyone.

'You see, when you open the door with the key still in the ignition, you hear the alarm. That reminds you not to forget the key. Haven't you ever seen that before?'

'Not exactly,' Brackett replied. 'I'm not very familiar with these newer models.'

He attempted a smile, gestured vaguely towards his own car as if that explained everything, and then peered through the tinted glass into the window of the Toyota and saw the key gleaming in the ignition. Watched by the boy, he then opened the door again, acknowledged the alarm and sat on the black upholstered bench seat. Before him, the steering wheel (now an italic *O*), the fascia, dials, a box of initials (*21 DNRP*) and a torn piece of turquoise cloth caught in the pincer grip of a broken windscreen wiper. Bracket left that where it was for the moment, then finally took it as if it were crystal, held it in his hand, felt the coldness of the silk, and placed it in his pocket. Blonde hair. Freckles. Turquoise dress. *Happens all the time.*

'You a cop?'

The boy's head was framed in the deckle-edge of the windscreen.

'No,' Brackett replied.

'Sure?'

'Yes.'

'Funny. I always recognize a cop.'

Brackett glanced up at the boy:

'You work here?'

'Uh-huh.'

'What's your name?'

'Billy Kent. What's yours?'

Brackett ignored that and got out of the car and silenced the din of the alarm. It was loud and he said so.

'Jap cars always are. It's weird that it still works.'

Brackett agreed, but whatever freak accident had made it so, he was grateful. The journey to Battery and Lingfield, it seemed, hadn't been wasted after all. Fifteen minutes earlier, when he first saw the Toyota, he had thought he was on the wrong track. That Mary Malewski was superfluous to the questions in his mind and that he should pack the whole damn thing up and go home. Not that he expected a yellow brick road, but he had expected something, for Brackett couldn't forget that there was, at least, one indisputable fact and to hell with Simmons. Loomis had wanted to tell him something and it wasn't just the time of day. He could still see him sitting on the bench gibbering about the dead girl; and more importantly he could see that moment, that split-second snapping of the head, the expression in the face when Brackett had said *Do you know me?*

Mary Malewski, however, was another matter. And for two reasons. First, a file had been stolen by person or persons unknown. And secondly, Brackett was convinced that whatever pieces of jigsaw there were (sky or no sky), they began to take shape in this very car next to him fourteen hours earlier.

He therefore turned back to the boy who was now leaning against the wire netting surrounding the compound, staring down at the docks. Brackett stood near him and offered him a cigarette which the boy accepted, commenting on the fact that it was English and lighting it as if it were touchpaper.

'Billy,' Brackett began casually, 'that Toyota wouldn't exactly be the ideal car to steal in the middle of the night, would it? I mean, if the key was in, someone opening the door is going to wake up half the neighbourhood.'

The boy nodded. Right.

'Well,' Brackett continued. 'Could you steal it *without* the key?'

'A Toyota like that? No way. Each key's numbered. Like in a bank vault, you know? I'm not saying it *couldn't* be done, like if you were an expert. But why risk it? You could steal a million cars in a tenth of the time.'

'The *owner* says the car was stolen.'

There was a sudden grin and the boy turned and looked at

Brackett, one hand pushing the hair back from his forehead.

'Well ... maybe there's always a first time. You know? But the guy who rips off that car has got to be pretty smart, right?'

'Right.'

'Got to know about engines. Ignition. Wiring. The whole works. Right?'

'Right.'

'So if he's so smart, how come he couldn't drive the mother? I mean – Jesus Christ, look at it. That's a heavy car. A guy's got to be insane to kill himself in that.'

'It wasn't a man who killed himself, Billy,' Brackett said quietly. 'It was a fourteen-year-old girl.'

Immediately and instinctively the boy laughed, then saw Brackett's expression and stared at him, a damson stain suddenly highlighting his cheeks, then finally he said, looking away:

'Oh, shit...'

'She's in the morgue now.'

'Shit.'

'They say *she* stole the car, Billy,' Brackett added, studying the back of the boy's head.

'No way, Mister.' The voice was emphatic, almost defiant. 'No way.'

Brackett nodded, touched the boy's arm and placed a ten-dollar bill in his pocket. Then he walked slowly back towards his car parked opposite the yard.

Mr Robert Plomer of Pacific Avenue was about to have a visitor.

7

Autofix, Welding
Autoline, Mtr Access.
Automatic Sprinkler Co. Ltd
Automatic Vending Equipmt
Automobeales, Gar.
Autonumis, Ltd
Autoprine Ltd, Mtl Finish Proc. & Pntg
Do
Autospray, Car Body Repairs
Autrey, J., Dr
Autrey, R.
Autumnal Landscp. Ltd
Autumn Flower, Restnt

'Autumn Glades. Can I help you, sir?'

'Yes. I understand you have a ... resident called Kemble staying there. A Mr H. Kemble.'

'One moment, sir... Kemble? Would that be Mr Harold Kemble?'

'Yes. I'm a friend and I just wanted to know how well he ... is.'

'One moment sir. I'll put you through to – Hallo? Are you still there, sir? Hallo?... *Hallo?*'

For those unfamiliar with San Francisco, Pacific Avenue is that richly embroidered headband that runs across the forehead of the city, from the golf-links to the Banking Centre, a distance of roughly two miles. Brackett approached this Parnassus from Grant Avenue, driving through the Chinatown of lantern slides, until he emerged on the peak of Nob Hill and beneath the shadow of the Golden Gate Bridge. Mr Robert Plomer, Brackett thought, was living within that shadow and always would. Even if he emigrated.

The exterior of the house was not remarkable, surprisingly, being white, two-storey, and as original as motel wallpaper. A Raleigh bicycle lay on the lawn, its rear wheel embedded in the earth beneath a eucalyptus. There were some rose bushes, a petite plaster statue of a dimpled cherub, two magnolia trees (no longer in flower), a mock Tudor door and a green Volkswagen. Assuming that this was a two-car family, the Volkswagen no doubt belonged to Plomer's wife.

Brackett rang the doorbell, and as he heard it chime the first bars of *The Bluebells of Scotland*, he realized immediately that the chances of finding a first edition of Yeats by the bedside table or a Cellini salt-cellar nudging the Wheaties was probably remote. The books would be chosen by the Literary Guild, the pictures by CBS, and the wine, no doubt, by Safeway. But Brackett was not there to carp; merely to gain an audience and then leave before the light faded. It was now six fifty-five and for some people the traditional diversions of Saturday evening had already begun.

'Yes?'

Brackett turned and found himself gazing down at the cider-skinned face of a woman whom he assumed to be one of those Filipinos that MacArthur had praised so highly, but who, unlike the General, had no intention of returning to anywhere west of Fisherman's Wharf.

'I'd like to speak to Mr Plomer. Is he at home?'

The woman hesitated and Brackett could already see the imaginary cord about to be hooked across the threshold, when he added:

'It's about his stolen car. The Toyota.'

'The Toyota?'

'Yes. This *is* Mr Plomer's house, isn't it?'

It was and Brackett was led into the hall and then abandoned beside a potted plant that looked as though it needed a drink as much as he did. He studied the decor (white walls decorated by a series of original prints home-made by the grubby fingers of a child) and listened to doors being opened and closed, a glimpse of another woman, presumably the wife, ginning a martini, until finally another pair of doors slid open at the end of the corridor and a man appeared from a den, his face registering familiar platitudes. *Now who do you think you are? Don't you think you could have phoned first? Do you realize we are expecting guests?* The list was infinite and Brackett side-stepped them all immediately by saying, as offhand as possible:

'Mr Plomer? Shall we talk here or in front of your wife?'

Plomer's reaction was automatic, and yet in a way, commendable. A mere freezing of the hand in mid-air, a slight opening of the mouth, but nothing more. Mr Robert Plomer, a man in his late forties and dressed in green corduroy trousers, open-neck striped shirt and natural suntan, had obviously been in training for this moment.

'May I ask who you are?' he said quietly, as if Brackett's own question had never existed.

'My name's Walter Brackett.'

'I know no one in the police called Brackett.'

'I didn't realize, Mr Plomer, that you were so familiar with the police.'

'I'm a lawyer and I have friends there.'

'So do I,' Brackett said. 'But I'm not from the police.'

It was possible that there was a flicker of relief in Plomer's eyes, and, if Brackett's instincts were correct, there should have been.

'Then you're from the insurance company?'

'No, Mr Plomer. I'm not from the insurance company.'

'Well, listen, I'm a very busy man and we do have guests arriving –'

'You didn't answer my first question.'

'I don't recall –'

'I asked whether we should talk here or in front of your wife?'

'I don't think we should talk anywhere, Mr Brackett,' Plomer said, still retaining a deceptive coolness. 'I think you should leave. Now if you'll excuse me. . .'

He began to walk towards the front door and Brackett allowed him to open it before he himself abruptly walked into the main room of the house, discovered with relief that the martini drinker was still there, and said as clearly as he could:

'Mrs Plomer?'

'Yes?'

The front door slammed and footsteps approached quickly.

'I apologize for interrupting, but my name is Walter Brackett. I'm a private investigator and I wonder if you could help me.'

In an oval mirror, Brackett could see Plomer appear, his mind rapidly debating the next move. Both Brackett's and his own.

'It's about a young girl who was found dead in your husband's car,' Brackett continued, keeping his back to the door. 'I wonder if by chance you might know who she was.'

The woman (thirty-five or so, beauty parlour features) lowered her glass, puzzled, and glanced at her husband.

'Helen,' Plomer said quickly, moving across the fake Persian carpet towards her. 'I've already talked to the police. The girl apparently stole my car.'

Brackett watched this domestic interlude patiently, a sliver of admiration for Plomer's style as he put his arm around his wife's waist.

'Mr Brackett has obviously been hired by the insurance company.'

Brackett ignored that and walked closer till he was standing in the centre of the room, and close enough to see the expression on the wife's face. She knew nothing at all, which was, as Brackett had been told, how it should be.

'Mr Brackett,' she said. 'Why would we know –'

'Her name is Mary Malewski. Does that mean anything?'

It didn't. As Brackett expected. But what he *didn't* expect was that it obviously didn't mean anything to her husband either, unless he was a better actor than Barrymore. Brackett repeated the name, this time looking directly at Plomer, and he could feel the house of cards he had so carefully erected between Battery and Pacific Avenue collapsing around him as emphatically as Samson's Temple. Mary Malewski was as remote to Plomer as a planet, and yet his initial behaviour demonstrated the opposite all too clearly. Square One. Unless –

'Unless she used another name.'

This time the ace hesitated in its descent. As did the knave.

Brackett needed just one more reaction, one small spur. Aware of Plomer's gaze, he fumbled idly in his pockets, saying:

'I have a picture of her somewhere. It might help,' and finally brought out a photograph the size of a postcard and was about to hand it over when Plomer said quickly:

'Mr Brackett – Helen is expecting guests.'

Brackett's hand froze, the photograph six feet away from them.

'Could we discuss this together in my den, Mr Brackett?' Plomer said. 'I'm sure I could give you any help you might need and it would allow my wife time to get ready.'

Plomer's face was anxious and his wife was curious, but Brackett was not a home-breaker, nor did he intend to be. He knew that Plomer would soothe his wife later with all the answers she needed to hear. They wouldn't be the right answers, but she would accept them with the same gratitude as she accepted the clothes, and the house on Pacific Avenue and the credit at Saks and Magnin's. The doubts would remain but this year, Helen, why don't we visit all those Greek islands you've always wanted to see. We could even hire a yacht.

Brackett returned the photograph to his pocket and said:

'Of course. It was thoughtless of me, Mrs Plomer. I'm sure your husband and I can straighten everything out. The girl undoubtedly is a total stranger.'

Plomer avoided Brackett's eye, refilled his wife's glass, kissed her cheek, then walked towards the corridor.

'This way, Mr Brackett.'

Brackett nodded and glanced at Plomer's wife.

'I trust I didn't spoil your evening, Mrs Plomer.'

There was no reply.

In the den, Plomer poured himself a drink. He didn't offer his guest one, but Brackett took it anyway on the grounds that since no one was paying his bills on the case, he'd grab his expenses at every opportunity he could get.

'You needn't have done that,' Plomer protested. He was referring, Brackett assumed, to Brackett's behaviour before Plomer's wife, and not to the stealing of the bourbon.

'I didn't want to, Mr Plomer. It was *your* choice.'

Plomer walked around Brackett then sat down in one of those black leather swivel-chairs that only the rich buy. And they all do. Brackett himself remained standing and discovered from one wall that Robert C. Plomer was an Elk (whatever that was), had stood next to Governor Reagan, played golf with a handicap, sat third from left at Yale, had a penchant for photographs by David Hamilton (overlit plates of underage girls) and collected models of elephants that dictated a passion either for pachyderms or his political party.

'Mr Brackett . . .' Plomer began.

'Before you say anything,' Brackett interrupted, 'I repeat I'm not from the police. Nor do I intend to inform them of your extra-marital affairs with a girl of fourteen who could not only wipe that legal grin from your diploma, but also put you in jail.'

'Now don't try and bluff me, Brackett –'

'Bluff you? If you weren't in the slightest bit guilty, you would have thrown me out ten minutes ago.'

'You've got no proof.'

'No. You're right. But I've got enough to put the matter in the hands of, say, the commissioner of police if I wanted to. Let's see what friendship does there.'

'Are you going to blackmail me, because –'

'No, Mr Plomer. I told you – I'm a private investigator. I haven't got my card but look it up in the book.'

'I've never heard of you.'

'*I* hadn't heard of *you* either. Until today.'

Plomer stared at Brackett, unsure. He was assessing the case, studying the jury – and then surprisingly, he gave in.

'I knew she should never have taken the car,' he said. And that was it.

'You didn't know her as Mary Malewski, did you?' Brackett asked.

'Who? No. Sally.'

'Sally what?'

'Sally. . . Sally Fitzgerald.'

'Sally Fitzgerald? That's a long way from Malewski.'

Plomer shrugged.

'It shouldn't be a crime, you know.'

'It isn't to me,' Brackett said. 'I just want to know who she is. I began with just a name. Now I've got two. So what I want you to do, Mr Plomer, is take me to where you stayed with her.'

'Now listen –'

'Motel?'

'No! It was –'

'What?'

A beat.

'Her room. But I just can't leave –'

'Yes, you can, Mr Plomer. Wait till tomorrow or the next day and who knows what some unscrupulous people can dig up. You're a lawyer and you know that better than me. So if you want to sit behind your desk on Monday, it's got to be now.'

'What about Helen?'

'You can tell her you had to identify your car.'

Plomer leant forward and stared at the sage-green carpet.

'The girl's lying in the morgue, Mr Plomer. But last night she was lying in a bed. I want to see that bed.'

'Do you promise that this won't get to the police?'

He was now scared and it showed.

'Not from me,' Brackett said. 'I'll promise you that.'

'It could destroy me –'

'Mr Plomer, if I wanted to hurt you, I could have done that just now in front of your wife. I'm only interested in the girl.'

A long pause, then:

'All right. I'll take you there. But first, could I have the photograph?'

'Of course, Mr Plomer.'

Brackett took out the picture and placed it neatly, face up, on the footstool. Plomer glanced at it then looked up at Brackett, his face stung with anger, and shouted:

'You bastard, Brackett. You fucking bastard!'

Brackett accepted the insult gracefully because he knew he deserved it. The photograph wasn't of Mary Malewski or Sally Fitzgerald or whoever she was because, as far as Brackett knew, there wasn't one. It was, in fact, a rather popular picture of

W. C. Fields that he had bought half an hour before in Union Square.

'Shall we go now, Mr Plomer?' Brackett said, walking to the door and opening it. 'Now that the games are over?'

8

'Is this it?' Brackett said.

Plomer nodded, sitting next to him in the car, sitting down low as if to be as inconspicuous as possible, He didn't need to be, for in that district of San Francisco no one cared what anyone else did, especially a simple case of petty adultery. Even the respectable swingers of Nob Hill would have considered that as passé as a rumble-seat.

'Believe me, Brackett, I didn't know she was so young.'

'Would it have made any difference?'

Plomer glanced at Brackett then slowly shook his head.

'All right,' Brackett said. 'Come on.'

Brackett stepped out of the Buick and on to the neon-lit sidewalk. It was a street of bars and assignations and one-way trips; the pathetic moonshine of crotch-barter and cock-roaching; of hookers and the hooked, where coke was never the real thing and babies entered the world with a *smack* and then left it later the same way. It wasn't one of Marlowe's mean streets. It was worse. The Age of Aquarius had finally attained its rancid majority right there.

'Are you sure the police will be kept out of this?' Plomer asked nervously for the twentieth time.

'Just show me the room. That's all.'

It was on the third floor above flights of stairs that were blessed only by the darkness. No one stopped them, no one asked questions, because no one probably cared. At one point, as they stepped over bottles and discarded newspapers, Brackett tried to visualize the stages, the mere quartet of years (for there could be no more) that had reduced a girl to the condition in which he had found her. But he couldn't. Perhaps it was the scar of his generation that he failed, but if that was so, then Brackett selfishly had no regrets. He recalled Horowitz saying once: 'It's not Vietnam we should defoliate, Walter. It's Turkey. And the B-52s shouldn't be sent west, but east. Just over Marseilles.' Over-dramatic rhetoric, of course, but the emotion was undeniable.

Plomer had now stopped before a door isolated at the end of a corridor. Below, in the hulk of the building, a television could be heard.

'Did she live alone?' Brackett asked.

'Yes. When she was here.'

'Do you have a key? The door's locked.'

A key was taken from the corner of a sash-window.

'Did *you* put it there last night?' Brackett asked.

'Yes. I always –'

'What time?'

'About . . . five o'clock.'

'How did you know she wasn't going to return?'

'I didn't. But I had to get back. Back home.'

'Yet you knew she had taken your car?'

'Yes . . . but I couldn't wait any longer. So I took a cab.'

'You're lucky you didn't get yourself mugged. Give me the key. I'll go in first.'

The door opened easily and Brackett stepped cautiously into the room. He wasn't expecting to find anyone there but old habits die hard. He then switched on the light and looked back at Plomer.

'Come in and close the door.'

Plomer hesitated then entered, saw the unmade bed, the sheets and pillows and turned immediately away, shaking, and tried to leave. Brackett grabbed hold of him and slammed him against a wardrobe as realization finally took over and Plomer began to tremble, babble to God, then he snapped, pressing his face against the wall. Any moment now, Brackett knew, he would probably cry but he wasn't yet cynical enough to deny him that. The girl, no matter what she was, deserved tears from someone.

Ignoring Plomer, Brackett checked the room. It didn't take long, for it revealed almost nothing. A small double bed, unwashed sheets, and a paperback copy of *The Exorcist* bookmarked by a tin-foil sheet of birth-pills (her period would have been due in four days) lying on the floor. A crumpled pair of tights. In the wardrobe were two dresses, a raincoat from Macy's, some shoes, two pairs of jeans, a handful of tee-shirts, a pair of soiled pants, a box of tampons, and all the wretched intimacies of her sex. But nothing to indicate who she was. There were no letters, no diary, nothing at all. It was as if she had wanted to live as anonymously as she died, and so far she had succeeded.

There were, mercifully, some attempts to add personality to this single room. Two posters had been taped to a wall. The first Brackett recognized as Marilyn Monroe (palomino hair, widow's eyes, the mouth of Suadella); the second he didn't, but it claimed to be of someone called *Janis*. Beneath this were some paper flowers in a jar set on the bedside table, accompanied, apart from a lamp, by a packet of Silva-Thins, some book matches with the word *Jimi's* on the cover, two magazines, a clock and a doll.

On another table was a record player (its tenant at the moment was David Bowie) and a tin of Band-Aid containing hash. There was also a small turquoise bag. Brackett's haste to open it, even to the extent of tipping the contents on to the floor, was, however, unnecessary, for it held nothing that a million other girls didn't possess: cigarettes, make-up, money, a Kleenex, a bottle of pills. That, on the whole, was the sum of it. Cul-de-sac.

Except for the snapshot.

Brackett laid the polaroid print on the record player for the moment and continued searching what little remained of the room. Plomer was now sitting on the edge of the bed smoking one of the Silva-Thins and looking as if he wanted the world to end. The tears had come and gone – the later ones being more for himself than the girl.

'Plomer?'

Brackett was flicking through a pile of magazines in a corner. Mostly juvenile glossies with hints on how to cope with dry hair and vaginal odour.

'Plomer, I'm talking to you.'

One or two movie magazines. *Screen Stories. Photoplay.* Things like that.

'Plomer – you'd better answer some questions then you can go home and dress for dinner.'

'There's nothing I can tell you.'

'Yes, you can. You called her Sally Fitzgerald. Is that the name she told you?'

'What do you mean – is that the name she told me?'

'You said she was called Sally Fitzgerald?'

'Yes.'

'Did you hear anyone else call her that?'

'Call her what?'

'Sally. Somebody might have said "Hallo, Sally" or "How are you doing, Sally?"'

'We didn't see anyone else.'

'You must have met her somewhere.'

'Of course I met her somewhere.'

'Where?'

'In a club.'

'What club?'

'I don't know,'

'This one?'

Brackett held up the bookmatches. *Jimi's.*

'Yes.'

'What was she doing there? Hustling?'

'No,' Plomer shouted indignantly. 'She was *not* hustling, as you call it.'

'She hustled *you.*'

'She *never* hustled me.'

'Don't tell me you didn't give her money.'

'What?'

'*Did* you give her money?'

'I may have...'

'Don't be coy, Mr Plomer. How much?'

'That's no business of –'

'How much?'

'I don't know...'

'Hundred dollars? Two?'

'No!'

'Fifty?'

'I can't remember. I don't keep count.'

'Of fifty dollars?'

'It might have been a hundred. I don't know...'

'You're burning the carpet.'

'What?'

'The carpet. You're burning it.'

Brackett walked across towards the sink. A mirrored cupboard contained some face cream, Bufferin, those sticks with cotton-wool on each end.

'So what did you talk about?' Brackett asked.

'Who?'

'You. What did you talk about?'

'Talk about?'

'Yes. Here. In this room. What the hell did you talk about?'

'We didn't talk about anything.'

'You just fucked?'

'Now, Brackett, I think I've had just about enough of your –'

'So be lucky you're not talking to the police.'

Plomer hesitated, his face flushed, then lit another cigarette and sat down again.

'Let's begin again,' Brackett said. 'What did you talk about?'

'Nothing much.'

'Give me some of that "nothing much".'

'It was just small talk.'

'I like small talk.'

'I can't remember every detail.'

'I thought lawyers were trained to remember details?'

'We were in bed. All right. What do people say in bed?'

'Tell me.'

'It was mostly about money.'

'Fine. Now we're getting somewhere.'

A tube of Alka-Seltzer. A nail-file. A can of deodorant and something for blackheads.

'But that's about all,' Plomer said. 'Some girl talk. She was worried about her figure... I don't know.'

'Did she talk about her past?'

'Not as far as I know.'

'She never said where she came from? Never mentioned anything about her past? No memories?'

'No. Believe me, she hardly said anything. She did once say she hated her parents. That's all.'

'She said that?'

'Yes. It was during an argument and she said I was behaving just like her father.'

'And she hated you for that?'

'She hated her father, I suppose.'

'She never . . . mentioned that she might want to find out where he was?'

'God no. I think that was the last thing she wanted. Why?'

'Nothing.'

Brackett smiled at the absurdity of it all. In a platonic way, he had behaved as idiotically as Plomer, believing the girl's wide-eyed desires to find her father and then falling for the paper-thin charm and giving her money. Maybe Kemble was right. Maybe he *should* take stock of his life.

'Why did she leave last night?' Brackett said.

'We had a fight.'

'What about?'

'It wasn't anything special.'

'Another man?'

'No.'

'Not another man?'

'No!'

'What then?'

'She wanted some more money.'

'How much?'

'Five hundred dollars.'

'Five – hundred – dollars?'

'Yes.'

'Did she say what for?'

'She said she was pregnant.'

'Did you believe her?'

'No.'

'So you refused to give her money?'

'Yes. I knew that she wanted it for something else.'

'Were you in bed while all this was going on?'

'Yes.'

'So what did she want it for? The five hundred dollars?'

'Look, she's dead –'

'Drugs?'

'Maybe.'

'Maybe?'

'All right. Yes!'

Brackett looked at him, then nodded and continued checking the room. The inventory was as unique as acne. Toothpaste. Toothbrush. A hairbrush with some of her hair still entangled in it. More pills (green and black), eye-shadow.

'So then she ran out?'

'Yes.'

'*Naked?* She ran into the street naked?'

'No –'

'You said you were in bed. I assumed –'

'She put on a dress.'

'While she was running out?'

'Yes.'

'Just a dress? No underwear?'

'No. She just grabbed her dress and ran out.'

'This colour?'

Brackett took out the torn piece of turquoise silk from his pocket. Plomer nodded and Brackett dropped it in the waste-basket.

'Didn't you try and stop her?' Brackett asked. 'While she was running out?'

'How could I?'

'Of course – you were naked too.'

'Look, she was screaming and trying to attract attention so I had to let her go.'

'What was she screaming about?'

'I don't know,' Plomer said. 'She said she'd get the money from somewhere else. That she had to.'

Brackett looked at him:

'Some*where* else or some*one* else?'

'Some*where* else. That's what she meant.'

'Any idea of the place she meant?'

'Plomer shook his head:

'No. It could be a dozen places within a block of here. Couldn't it? You don't have to be blind to see that.'

Brackett nodded. Yes.

'So then,' he said, 'after she left the bed, she pulled on the dress. What else?'

'What else what?'

'What else did she take?'

'Some shoes I think. And the car keys.'

'You let her take those?'

'I told you, I couldn't stop her. But believe me, if I knew what was going to happen, I *would* have stopped her no matter what the consequences.'

Brackett stared at him but made no comment.

'Did she often use your car?'

'Not often.'

Brackett pointed to the turquoise bag.

'That's hers, isn't it?'

'Yes.'

'And she left that?'

'Yes.'

'Just her dress, shoes and the keys?'

'Yes. How many times?'

'Because the police found my card in your car.'

Plomer looked at Brackett, puzzled:

'Your card?'

'Yes,' Brackett said. 'My business card. That's what puzzles me.'

'What kind of card?'

'An ordinary business card. Brackett & Kemble.'

Plomer suddenly opened his mouth wide and said:

'*That's* where I heard your name before. Brackett. A private investigator.'

It was now Brackett's turn to be on the wrong end of the see-saw.

'You *knew* the card was there?'

'It's been there for about three months. I never really took any notice.'

'Why not? *You* didn't put it there, did you?'

'No, but a lot of people drive my car. My assistant drives my car.'

'But that doesn't explain why you didn't take any notice of the card.'

'I'm a lawyer, Brackett. We hire private detectives all the time.'

Brackett could already hear the balloon deflating.

'You never hired *us*,' he said bitingly, trying to regain status.

'I'd never heard of you. Are you a *new* firm?'

Brackett let that pass and concentrated on the wardrobe. So the acorn had been explained, but he wished there had been a different reason for planting it. Such as Loomis. But the girl had simply visited him when she did, taken his card that he had offered and left it in her lover's car. Simple as that.

Plomer stood up.

'Any more questions, Brackett?'

'Yes,' Brackett replied forcefully. A *new* firm? Where had the man *been* all his life! 'Sit down, Plomer!'

'My wife's going to start asking –'

'That's your problem. Remember I'm doing you a favour. Now, I want to know about other men this girl knew.'

'What other men?'

'Don't make it difficult or I'll keep you here all night.'

Plomer sat down.

'Did she ever talk about her other lovers?' Bracket asked.

'Never.'

'But there *were* other lovers, weren't there?'

A pause.

'Plomer, you're an intelligent man. A lousy lawyer, perhaps, but an intelligent man. So tell me about the other men.'

'I didn't ask.'

'Never?'

'What was the use? I knew she'd lie.'

'But you knew?'

'Yes...'

The tone in Plomer's voice said everything. He might even have loved the girl, but the terms were obviously hers.

'Many?' Brackett asked.

'I don't know. But there were. You just can't sleep with someone, be ... close to someone and not know. Can you?'

'Let's hope your wife doesn't think the same way.'

The remark was below the belt and regretted, and Brackett considered apologizing but he never was capable of such an act, even to Dorothy. That, he knew, was partly why she had left him when she did. As well as the other things.

'Now, before you go – I want you to tell me about this.'

Brackett had taken the polaroid print from the record player and was holding it in his hand. It was of the girl and she was naked. It wasn't a good picture, neither erotic nor artistically posed. It merely depicted a young girl standing before a mirror and in such a way that one could not only see the front of the girl's body, but also her back. The subject however wasn't doing anything that was even mildly obscene, unless one considered *any* photograph that shows a nude girl of fourteen obscene. Brackett himself, in fact, found it rather attractive in an amateurish way, though Lolita had never been exactly his style.

'Did *you* take it?' he asked.

'No.'

'Look at it.'

'I said I didn't take it.'

'It *is* of the girl you knew as Sally Fitzgerald, isn't it?'

'Yes.'

'But you didn't take it?'

'Look, Brackett,' Plomer said angrily, 'I know you don't think much of me, but I never took that. It's not my kind of ... of fun.'

'But you've seen it before?'

'Yes. Once.'

'She showed it to you?'

'Yes. She liked it. It flattered her.'

'But she never said who took it?'

'No.'

There was nothing more to say.

'Good-bye, Plomer. You'd better get home to your guests.'

Plomer stood up, almost reluctantly, it seemed.

'You think I was a fool, don't you?' he said.

'No. No, I don't think anything. Goodnight. And I assure you, you'll never hear about this again.'

Brackett heard Plomer say 'Thank you' but he didn't reply.

He merely watched as Plomer gazed around the room once more, placed a fallen pillow back on to the bed, then hurried out of the room, back to the white walls and the martinis of Pacific Avenue.

From the window, Brackett could see the street below and the lights. One of them spelt out *Jimi's* and five minutes earlier he would probably have gone there and asked more questions, but not now. Not any more. He didn't care if he was about to discover that the dead girl was a President's daughter for he was about to draw the line. Enough was enough.

Having thought that, he realized he wasn't fooling anyone, including himself, for the speech wasn't even worthy of Pilate. He was committed, because if he gave up now he might as well select his wicker chair next to Kemble, pick up a comic-book and hand his room-and-board back to Liebermann. He was committed, not only because it was the only thing he knew (talented or not), but because the polaroid photograph was still in his hand and he had just seen something else that he had overlooked – the cynosure of pale pink skin having almost robbed him of the full value of the composition.

In using the mirror device (not original but effective), the photographer had realized that unless he stood at an angle to the girl, he too would be seen in the mirror. This he had achieved successfully leaving only the shadow of an arm. However, he was not alone, for a third person had been in the room, and whose knowledge of the photographer's tricks was obviously lacking, since a face, a mere blur but a face nevertheless, was visible almost like a mirage behind the left shoulder of the girl. A witness to the act, unrecognizable in the millimetres before Brackett. But millimetres could easily become centimetres. Or even metres.

In Danny's Arcade, as Brackett was well aware, it happens all the time.

The pusher should never have gone to the cinema. That was his first mistake. He also shouldn't have sat in the centre row. That was his second. He had only himself to blame, therefore, when he felt the sharp point of a knife pressing into the nape of his neck and heard a voice say below the soundtrack:

'Pick up your popcorn, Baby. The car's outside.'

'It'll cost you two-fifty.'

'It used to be a dollar.'

'*Nothing* used to be a dollar. Even a dollar.'

'So how big could you blow it up?'

'What is it?'

Brackett handed the photograph across the counter. Around him, he was surrounded by a gallery of images the size of Chesterfield sofas; some famous (Bogart, Dean, Dillinger, the Son of God), some frivolous, some anonymous (godsons, little sisters, Vietnam Veterans) and some simply faces in a crowd. Behind him, fruit machines, pinball machines and the expectant gaze of Saturday night.

'That'll be five dollars.'

'You just said two-fifty.'

'For beaver shots, it's five.'

'What do you mean – "beaver shots"?'

'You English?'

'When I want to be.'

'Five dollars.'

'Look, forget the girl. I just want an enlargement of the right-hand corner.'

A slow raising of the head, a pursing of the mouth, then the shrug:

'Okay. *Four* dollars for the girl. The whole bojangles. Who cares?'

'I said I don't want the girl. Just the right-hand corner.'

'You win. Are you happy now? You won. *Three* dollars.'

It took ten minutes and Brackett was presented with an enlargement big enough to see every freckle and scar on the girl's body. It wasn't an expert job, but it was sufficient. Brackett not only had an almost life-size reproduction of the dead girl, but also a close-up of a familiar face smiling at him from behind the girl's back. Brackett paid the money, rolled up the still-damp photograph and called Horowitz. He was out. Instead he found himself obliged to talk to Henderson.

'Sergeant Henderson? Walter Brackett. I'd like to ask you –'

'Wait a minute, Brackett. This is the morgue, not the Hollywood Squares.'

'Henderson,' Brackett said into the phone. 'It's about the girl. Mary Malewski. Remember?'

'How can I forget? We're now working on her teeth. Any clues?'

'Patience, sergeant. But I want to ask you about the boy who works in the pound. The one on Lingfield and Battery. Know him?'

'Billy Kent? Sure.'

'He wouldn't be still there now, would he?'

'This time? No. Closes at seven.'

'Well, do you know where he'll be?'

'Billy? Probably at a gym. That's where he usually hangs out.'

'Any particular gym?' Brackett asked.

'Listen, Brackett. I thought you guys knew everything. The old gumshoe bit. That's how you do it on tee-vee, ain't it? The –'

'Sergeant –'

'– blonde, the gun, and the asshole of a dog –'

'Sergeant – all I want is the name of the gym.'

A sudden pause then Henderson said:

'So find it your fucking self.'

And the phone was put down. Brackett listened to the dead signal for a moment, then replaced the receiver. Billy Kent. The boy who knew all about cars. Billy Kent.

Brackett shrugged, picked up the rolled-up photograph and manoeuvred his way to the street.

It was now dark.

Suddenly the rear wheels began to slide in the sand, then gripped as the car was thrust forward and the lights lit up the beach, a swathe of white, and then it lurched into rock-pools and drove for the cabin. Tyres slid sideways, regained their momentum and the woman was seen for the first time running, a stark silhouette, running in panic, turning back then forward, then finally finding her only escape in the sea itself. She was seen to run, stumble, and then try to swim, but the tide was low and the car was already in the water spraying a cascade of surf around her and stopping, doors opening.

She didn't move, but stood and turned almost arrogantly, a Liberty statue in the waves, turned full face into the headlights and waited, hand outstretched, as if she were a Society hostess on a pillared terrace ready to greet the first guest of the Season.

'That's her,' the pusher said to the man behind him. 'That's Norma Wheatley.'

'Thank you, Baby.'

9

One day, Brackett thought wearily, he ought to make a count of all the gyms in San Francisco as a kind of therapeutic exercise. He estimated that he had visited nine, all of whom had heard of Billy Kent, but none had seen him. Brackett visited one or two bars as well, but that was merely to ease himself into the evening. After an hour, he ran out of gas in the middle of Market Street and had to walk two blocks before he could get the Buick started again. He also found he was running out of money (it had been a bad day for gratuities) and hoped that he would find someone who would talk without demanding an advance. Billy Kent, when Brackett eventually found him in a basement in Tippett Street, fortunately had a heart of gold.

As soon as Brackett entered the gym (a small flight of stone steps, two sets of green swing doors, and posters still advertising the fight between Liston and Ali), he realized that he had been there before. It had been a long time ago, perhaps twenty years, when it was Marciano and Sugar Ray and the last agonized outcries of Louis as the *banderillas* of age finally eclipsed his career.

Nothing had changed except the clientelle. It was the same sweat, the same smell, the same red-painted wooden tier on the right where senescent hopefuls had sat, their minds sparring with Graziano and Billy Conn, sitting apart from each other on the wooden slats and staring ahead as yet another black boxer sniffed and shuffled in the ring before them. They sat there now, in overcoat and hat, never moving for hours, staying because this was all they knew and they had nowhere else to go. Once Brackett had sympathized (and in a way he still did) and knew their names, and they would talk of the 'big fights' that never really existed. Some could remember seeing the Long Count and those who didn't knew every punch, every feint, every gesture of each round.

Behind the tiers, on the wall, were framed photographs, some signed, but few of fighters. They were actors and second-billing comedians, singers and Italian restaurateurs. They hadn't changed either, except that the ink had faded and the names were forgotten.

In a corner was an office. At least, it was two hardboard walls shutting off the fading optimism of the basement and containing a desk, a telephone, random pin-ups of women and men, and an old man in a polka-dot bow tie who was still alive and known, since he was born in Brooklyn, as 'Dixie'.

As Brackett entered the partition door, the old man turned and saw him, a dead cigar in his mouth, double-took, then held up both hands. He hadn't changed. He was still bald, still half-blind and still, if Brackett's memory was correct, wearing the same waistcoat.

'Don't tell me,' Dixie said immediately, his eyes widening behind his bifocals. 'A face, I never forget.'

Pause, index finger rising, then:

'Harry Kemble!'

Brackett smiled.

'Wrong end of the horse, Dixie. Walter Brackett.'

'*Wal*-ter Brackett. How could I forget? Walter Brackett. Still in the hotel business?'

'That was Harry's old man. I never was –'

'Gave it up? Well, Walter, I always say – if you can't have the Fairmont or the St Francis, forget it. Conrad Hilton. Now *he* was a clever boy. Buys the Plaza Hotel, New York. Do you know how many people realize when they shell out the peas to stay in the Plaza Hotel, New York, that they're really staying in a New York Hilton? And an old one at that. That makes you think, doesn't it?'

'I think Sonesta own it now, Dixie –'

'What?'

'Nothing,' Brackett said.

Dixie stared at him as if he were in small print, then said:

'So what you doing, Walter? Have a seat. Use the desk.'

'I'm looking for a boy called Billy Kent.'

'Billy Kent?'

Dixie didn't look at him but Brackett could see that he now remembered what Brackett was.

'He's a good boy.'

'I'm not saying he isn't, Dixie. I just want to know where he is.'

'A good boy. A good fighter. A few more pounds and he could be a heavyweight.'

'Is he here, Dixie?'

The cigar was rolled slowly between finger and thumb and then:

'In the locker room. Getting changed.'

Brackett moved away from the desk when Dixie said anxiously:

'Walter? Don't lose me a fighter, will you?'

Brackett smiled, shook his head and walked across the gym and into the locker room. The description was euphemistic for it was no more than a broken-tiled shower, a bench and a single barred window. When Brackett entered, Billy Kent had his back to him, zipping up a small canvas bag.

'Hallo, Billy,' Brackett said, closing the door.

The boy turned quickly, saw Brackett (a flicker of caution in his eyes, his shoulders already on the defence), then he recognized him, snapped his fingers and said:

'The car freak? At the pound.'

'Right.'

'You a fighter?'

'No.'

'You could have been. The way you stand.'

Billy seemed relaxed but Brackett could sense the tension as the boy casually placed the canvas bag on the bench, talking, marking time and leaving his hands free.

'I just want to talk to you.'

'About the Toyota?'

'No, Billy. About a girl. This one.'

Brackett showed him the polaroid print. The enlargement remained rolled up on the front seat of his car. Brackett studied the boy's face as he held up the photograph towards the light bulb, a stage-managed frown.

'Know her?' Brackett said.

The photograph was tossed aside.

'Never seen her before.'

'Never?'

'Never. Who is she? Miss America?'

'You tell me. You were there when the photograph was taken.'

A tension and the boy looked up, pushing aside his hair.

'Who says so?'

'I do.'

Brackett watched him stand up, raising his body on his toes, measuring him.

'You know, I think I could lay you out,' the boy said.

'Probably. But you were still there when this photograph was taken. Look at the picture again. That's *your* face in the mirror, isn't it?'

'You sure you're not a cop?'

'Positive. I just want your help, that's all.'

'Legit?'

'What else?'

'That's a new one. You a friend of Dixie's?'

'For twenty years. Ask him.'

A frown. Then:

'All right. What are you looking for?'

'Who's the girl?'

Billy picked up the picture again, then grinned, smacking the photograph with the back of his hand.

'Great pair of tits. Right?'

'What's her name?'

'Her? Jean.'

'Jean?'

'Yeh.'

'Are you sure?'

'You asked me her name and it's Jean. What do you think she's called? Rocky?'

'Jean what?'

'Jean Harlow.'

'Jean *Harlow*? Now come on, Billy. Just tell me her name.'

'I told you her name. Jean Harlow. That's her name.'

He repeated it twice and he meant it.

'Jean Harlow was a film actress,' Brackett said.

'So is this girl. Not in films. But she's an actress. Know what I mean?'

'Jean *Harlow*?'

'Listen, she told me her name was Jean Harlow. Maybe there are two of them.'

Brackett sighed. Jean Harlow. He could see Henderson's face now.

'Billy, she told me her name was Mary Malewski. She told someone else it was Sally Fitzgerald. Now you're telling me it's Jean Harlow.'

There was a laugh:

'I believe it. I believe it all.'

'Why do you believe it?'

The boy hesitated, then shrugged:

'Aw, shit. She makes up all kinds of names. You know? Like she's crazy. But what the hell?'

'Did you know her well?'

A shrug. Eyes flicking away.

'Yeh. Kind of. She wanted to be my old lady but . . . you know. I'm a fighter, right?'

'That costs money,' Brackett said. 'Equipment, promotion. . .'

'I manage.'

'Did *she* give you money?'

'Jean? No. . .'

A grin.

'Well, yeh. A little. You know? Groupie talk.'

'Where'd she get it?'

Billy glanced at him:

'You're not going to bust her, are you?'

'No, Billy. She's dead. She was the girl in the Toyota.'

Silence. Billy didn't move, but stared at Brackett for a long time, then slowly sat on the bench in profile. In the gym could be heard the shuffle of feet on canvas, a shout of advice, and someone tried the locker-room door, but Brackett leant on it till they swore and walked away. He lit a cigarette and offered one to the boy, but it was ignored.

'I'm sorry, Billy, it's true.'

'The fucking kid. The stupid, fucking kid!'

He didn't cry like Plomer. In fact he didn't do anything except swear at the girl and stare into space. Brackett sat next to him on the bench, almost a sinister echo of the scene with Loomis. Except that this boy cared more, even though he didn't show it.

'Billy . . . who took the photograph?'

There was no reply, so Brackett placed the picture on his lap.

'Billy . . . she's dead and I want to find out about her. Who took the photograph?'

Slowly the boy turned his head and studied Brackett, then said:

'Are you on the level?'

'Yes.'

'I mean with me. Because I don't want any hassle with the cops, you know?'

'You have my word.'

'That doesn't mean – aw, shit, what's your name?'

'Walter Brackett.'

'You got an old lady?'

'Did have. But she died.'

'That's the way it goes, isn't it?'

'Tell me about the girl, Billy.'

'Jesus fucking Christ. . .'

An intake of breath. Then:

'Well . . . like she used to hustle these old guys. I mean, what she told me, some of them were sick, man. And . . . well. . . They never knew she was under age, right? Maybe some did, but . . . well. . .'

'Did you know any of them?' Brackett said.

'No. She didn't want to talk about them. And I never asked. I mean, like she told me *about* them but not who they were. Shit, I tried to stop her but she was popping, right?'

'What?'

'Anything. Coke, speedballs, smack. . . She said it kept her together.'

The boy shrugged despairingly.

'So, who took the picture, Billy?'

'He was . . . well, he didn't want to screw her, you know? He just wanted to watch. Well, maybe he couldn't. I don't know – ah, fucking shit. Do you mind if we get outta here?'

'Sure. I've got a car outside. I'll give you a lift.'

Brackett opened the door and waited as Billy picked up the canvas bag. The boy looked frail and very young.

'Mister – you're not putting me on about –'

'No. I had to identify her. She's dead.'

'Maybe it's for the best, huh? I mean, what kind of life did she have? Lately, I don't think *she* knew who she was.'

'Come on, Billy.'

They walked across the gym. Brackett noticed Dixie watching but he didn't say anything. As they reached the street, Billy stopped and leant against the wall, breathing deeply at the night air.

'You know something?' he said. 'I was going to see that poor chick tonight. Saturday night. The big kaboodle. Banga banga bang. . .'

'Billy,' Brackett said, taking the photograph he was still holding in his hand. 'Who took the picture?'

'A cop.'

The answer was as emphatic as it was startling.

'A *cop*?'

'Yeh.'

'I can't believe that. He'd never say he was a cop even if he was.'

'He didn't have to, mister. I can recognize a cop a million miles away. I don't make mistakes.'

'You made a mistake with me.'

'The exception to the rule. Isn't that what they say?'

'You're saying that the man who took this picture was a cop?'

'Right. Everything about him. Not physically, but I could smell it. Like in the ring, after the first round when the bell goes, you know everything there is about the other guy if you're smart. Everything. From the size of his shoes to how many kids he's got. And you know if you're going to lose or going to win. And if you're going to win, you know *when* you're going to win. Ali doesn't give out bullshit when he raps to the press because he has one advantage over all of us. He fights the first round before he puts on his jock-strap. I ain't got that yet, but I'm learning. I learnt about cops since I was this high. I know who's on the side of the law and who's not. I *know*. That's a fact.'

'So all right. You think he was a cop.'

'Think? I'd *swear* to it.'

'What did he look like?' Brackett said.

'I couldn't say... It was dark and I only saw him for a minute. But he was about forty-five, I guess. No, maybe older. I don't know. In a suit.'

'Did he speak at all?'

'No. Not much. He told me to get lost.'

'Did you know his name?'

Billy laughed.

'Oh, sure. He had a name but it could have been Mary Poppins. He *said* he was called Hal Jordan.'

'Al Jordan?'

'Al or Hal. What the fuck.'

'Hal Jordan?' Brackett said. 'That doesn't sound like a name you just think up.'

'So maybe it's another movie star. Like Jean Harlow.'

'Maybe.'

It had now begun to rain (that Bay Area rain that falls like gravity) as they began to walk south along Tippett Street. The boy now seemed restless, edgy, glancing around him, but the street itself was empty, even at that time of night.

'Billy,' Brackett said, trying to keep pace with him. 'This Hal Jordan. Did you see him again?'

'No. Only that once. I didn't even know it was him until she told me.'

'But you'd heard of him?'

'Oh, sure. You talk to any junkie and they've heard of him. He's their Mr Moses. Know what I mean?'

'You mean he supplies them?'

'Right. But no one's ever seen him.'

'*You* did. And so did the girl.'

Billy stopped and looked quickly around him and said:

'Shit, man. Don't you think I *know* that?'

'And that scares you?'

'No. Yes – well, this sounds crazy, but I feel kind of safe working at the pound. All those cops hanging around...'

He looked away, almost shyly.

'Yes. I'm scared.'

A pause.

'Billy,' Brackett said. 'Was he white or black?'

'Jordan? White.'

'You sure?'

'Sure I'm sure.'

Brackett nodded.

'Let's get in the car,' he said. 'It's raining.'

'No thanks. I'll split here. I just got two blocks.'

The boy began to back away.

'Billy – before you go. When was the last time you saw ... Jean. The girl?'

'Last night.'

'You saw her *last* night? Where?'

'In Jimi's in North Beach.'

'Wait a minute.'

'Look – I don't like streets. They make me nervous. Another time.'

'Give me one more minute.'

Brackett moved into a darkened shop doorway. It smelt of urine and drunks. Billy hesitated, sighed, then huddled into a corner.

'Are you trying to get Hal Jordan?' he asked.

'I wasn't. But I think I'll keep it in mind.'

'Forget it.'

'Billy,' Brackett said, ignoring the remark. 'What time was she in Jimi's last night?'

'Jean? I don't know.'

'Well, was it late or early?'

'Late. Yeh. Late.'

'Very late?'

'Yeh. About four o'clock.'

'Did you talk to her?'

'No. She just ran in. She looked kind of wild, you know.'

'And then she left?'

'Right.'

'Alone?'

'No. With this guy. He's a kind of contact. A runner, you know?'

'Of Jordan's?'

'Yeh. Right.'

'And she left with him?'

'Yeh. She went to the john, then she left. After about ten minutes.'

'This man – had you seen him before?'

'Oh sure. Lots of times.'

'You wouldn't know his name, would you?'

'You ask a lot of questions.'

'So I've been told. The man's name?'

'Joe. Big City Joe.'

'Big City Joe? That's his name?'

'Right. Big City Joe.'

'Well, didn't he have another name? Like Kent?'

'Sure. Everybody does.'

'It wasn't Loomis, was it?' Brackett asked.

'Yeh,' Billy said, staring up at him. 'Yeh. Loomis. Say, how did you know that?'

'Just putting things together, that's all,' Brackett said. 'But you're *sure* it was Loomis last night? About forty, wears a suit and tie, regular haircut, gold cuff-links –'

'Yeh. Loomis. Hangs around Sausalito.'

'Billy – you couldn't tell me someone at Jimi's who might have seen them both as well?'

'They won't talk to you. That's for sure.'

'Name one. Just to see.'

A sigh.

'Well, there's this Jamaican called Murray. Big black mother. He's always there. But keep me out of it.'

'I will. Thanks.'

Billy moved out of the darkness and looked quickly up and down the street.

'If you hear anything more,' Brackett said. 'Dixie knows where I am.'

Billy looked at Brackett, grinned, then he was gone. Brackett stood in the doorway until he could no longer hear the boy's footsteps, then tried to assess the events of the day, and more particularly of the last hour. If he was to believe Billy Kent (and he saw no reason why he shouldn't), he was now involved with the death of Loomis whether Simmons, Johanssen and the whole pack of them liked it or not. It hadn't been his intention (at least not consciously so), but, in all honesty, he had no regrets. For, from the very beginning he had known that it wasn't Mary Malewski, unknown girl from nowhere, that he was interested in. It was Joseph Loomis. Big City Joe. That was more his style. That was more worthy of Brackett & Kemble. Monday, he thought, he'd have some cards printed. Plain and simple. Just two words: *Walter Kemble*. Nothing more.

The Buick was isolated by a street light (a rectangle of dry asphalt on one side), and, as he walked towards it, he suddenly felt wide awake and refreshed, eager for the night. Brackett got in the car, sat behind the wheel, and as he reached for the gear shift, his hand touched something cold that moved and then rolled slowly on to the floor.

He turned and saw that it was the poster-size photo of the girl staring up at him as the picture unravelled, almost teasingly exposing her. Brackett stared at it, and his stomach tightened as he realized that it wasn't only Loomis he was concerned with; it was someone called Hal Jordan.

Someone who was very much alive, and who was not only a murderer but also, according to Billy Kent, a cop. He could be forgiven, therefore, if his nerves were tense, the greyhound in the slips, as the implication of this hit him. He could also be forgiven if these nerves affected his imagination and he believed he was being followed as he drove back down Tippett Street towards his office. That black Ford Sedan behind him was as innocent as a babe in Limbo, a latent product of the amateur paranoia he had abandoned two decades ago. The driver was simply going downtown, just as Brackett was; going to the hurdy-gurdy of the bars and the clubs and the noise.

After all, it *was* Saturday evening.

When Brackett reached the office, it was nine o'clock; the Ford was no longer in sight and Liebermann was about to close the delicatessen for the night. The Hungarian had read all about the crime in the streets, had seen what happened to the bit-players on television and was taking no chances.

'Any messages for me, Mr Liebermann?' Brackett asked, walking towards the stairs.

'I put it under the ashtray, Mr Brackett.'

Twenty-five years and they still addressed each other as if they were a double act in vaudeville.

'You mean someone called?' Brackett asked.

'Yes, Mr Brackett.'

'Who?'

'A woman, Mr Brackett. I wrote it down and put it under the ashtray.'

Brackett thanked him and entered his room. It was unlocked, as always, in case he received, as someone once said, 'a patient client'. Brackett closed the door, switched on the desk-lamp and looked at the piece of greaseproof paper. This time it was adequately legible and Liebermann was right. Brackett *had* received a call. Two calls in fact, and both from the same party. He read the poignant message, then screwed it up and threw it in the waste-basket. Mrs Markstein and her lost dog would just have to learn to live apart for a while.

After a shower, Brackett changed back into the same clothes, put the remainder of his piggy-bank into his wallet, filled a tumbler with whiskey, sat behind his desk and looked at his notes on Loomis. He read them through twice, especially the conversation in the morgue, then underlined the words 'back seat'. What had seemed like gibberish before, now began to make a little more sense. It was still, of course, gibberish, still the babbling of a frightened man sitting in the apparent sanctuary of a police precinct. But some things could be surmised.

It was, let's face it, Brackett himself who had assumed that Loomis had been on the bridge simply because he wanted to jump; he had thought that had been a clever deduction, but it wasn't, for Loomis had told him, face to face, that he was in the Toyota. Not only that, but that he had been in the back seat not the front. And the rear of the car had been undamaged. But then, why was he frightened? What had he seen? His written statement to the police perhaps could clarify that, but Brackett doubted it. Not if Hal Jordan, his employer, was a cop himself and in a position to read it. That would have ensured Loomis's death before he signed on the dotted line. And so he had gabbled it out to Brackett. Or at least some of it. The rest he was going to tell later. Except, of course, that someone got to him first.

Brackett wrote all that down on a clean sheet of paper, added a few questions, one or two possible answers, and then wrote down *Hal Jordan*. In fact he wrote down *Hal Jordan* three times. Like this:

Hal Jordan
Hal Jordan
Hal Jordan

He also instinctively wrote another name underneath, then crossed it out quickly because such doodling was dangerous.

After drinking another whiskey to give his liver something to play with, Brackett picked up the city telephone directory, found one or two Jordans, checked them out, (including a florist, a cab driver and a rabbi), then pushed the book aside. Jordan was a pseudonym. Naturally, it had to be. Finally, with his mind ringing changes, he went to the Buick and returned with the rolled-up photograph and taped it to the wall opposite the door.

Brackett stood in front of it as the photographer had done, as if some extra-sensory power would furnish him with an identity. But all he saw was a picture of a nude girl and the face of Billy Kent smiling out at him and nothing more.

The telephone rang. It was Herb Johanssen.

'Walter? Herb.'

Brackett sat on the edge of the desk, keeping the photograph before him.

'Hallo, Herb,' he said.

'So how's things?'

'So so. You?'

'Oh, you know... Look, Walter, I just called to say I'm sorry about today. Not helping you get the pass and that –'

'That's all right, Herb. I've forgotten all –'

'I mean, you really must think I'm a shit –'

'Herb, will you stop going on about that,' Brackett said, irritated. 'Just forget it.'

'Well . . .' the voice diminished, 'I just wanted to tell you that. And see how you got on – at the pound?'

'Oh, fine, Herb. Fine.'

'That's good. Fine, huh?'

'Yes, Herb. Fine.'

'Good. . .'

'You?'

'Oh, we're up to here, Walter. Simmons has been talking to every screwball in town.'

'No leads?'

'No. . .'

'Too bad,' Brackett said, unconvincingly, almost smiling to himself. 'Well, Herb, it's been nice talking to you –'

'If there's anything I can do –'

Brackett stared at the photograph, hesitated, then said:

'Yes, there is, Herb. You don't know anyone called Hal Jordan, do you? Could be a cop.'

There was a long pause and Brackett thought the phone had been cut off.

'Herb? You there?'

'Yes. Jordan did you say?'

'Yeh.'

'No. . . But then I don't know every rookie in San Francisco.'

'This is no rookie. Anyway, it was just a wild hope. Bye, Herb.'

Brackett then held the receiver in his hand until he heard the click and put it down. His eyeline was now centred on the face of Dorothy, then he turned away and reached for his coat. As he put it on, he suddenly began to feel nervous again. Not fearful or apprehensive, but more like a boy on his first date. It sounded an absurd description, but that's exactly what it was. Perhaps for that reason, Brackett decided to call Horowitz. Just in case.

'Sidney? Walter –'

'Oh, Walter,' Horowitz said, his voice out of breath. In the background, Brackett could hear voices and someone shouting for coffee. 'I can't talk to you now. Something's come up about the girl.'

'You know who she is?'

'All I know is that Homicide's in a panic. Just a minute. What? I'll be right there. Walter – I've got to go.'

'Sidney – wait a minute. Meet me later, can you?'

'I can't – look, if I can I will. Where?'

'At Jimi's. Know it?'

'Yeah. Bye, Walter.'

Brackett put down the phone, stood staring at it for a moment, then switched off the light and hurried downstairs.

Liebermann was behind the counter adding up the day's takings as Brackett entered the delicatessen.

'If anyone wants me, Mr Liebermann,' he said, 'I'll be here.'

Brackett wrote down *Jimi's Club* on a piece of paper, then said:

'You can bolt the door after I leave, Mr Liebermann. I'll use the side entrance when I come back. It could be very late.'

'Yes, Mr Brackett. Goodnight, Mr Brackett.'

Outside in the street, it was still raining, but the sky was clearing. Brackett thought for a moment that he should have taken the gun from his desk, but that appeared melodramatic, and besides, the licence had expired. And so he got into the Buick and drove away.

At Market Street, the black Ford reappeared in the rear-view mirror. And stayed there.

10

Cushions. The main floor of the club seemed to be covered with cushions the size of pool tables, overlapping each other, jostling for space like lily-pads suffocating the surface of an ornamental pond. Cushions and bodies, lying, sex against sex, some sleeping, some entwined in the propriety of an embrace, some merely daydreaming. Cushions and bodies and noise, an incessant backbeat, a strata of amplified sound punctuating the darkness and upstaging everything and everyone. What light there was was not for reading or writing letters home to mother, but mere appendices to the gloom, sufficient to allow the waitresses (California blondes in tee-shirt and jeans. Just as Brackett had seen Mary Malewski) to serve the drinks without stepping on a thigh or a lock of hair. There were no go-go dancers, no female Bajazeths pistoning their bottoms in cages, no bunny tails, none of that tourist honey. Just a large attic room for digital conversations and private thuribles of dope.

In decor, Jimi's wasn't the Sistine Chapel or Versailles, and no one wanted it to be, or even cared. It was there to serve a purpose, illegal perhaps, and in that it succeeded. As Brackett stood at the entrance, adjusting his eyes and gazing at the acres of denim and the plantations of hair, he felt as conspicuous as a dodo and just about as extinct. He was also unwelcome.

'That's as far as you go, Charlie. This club is strictly exclusive.'

Brackett turned towards something that claimed by its shirt to have been born under the sign of Taurus and looked as though it had been trampled in the process.

'I'm looking for someone,' Brackett said, staring over the man's head.

'Aren't we all?' the man replied. 'There's the door.'

Brackett lowered his gaze ten inches and said, as casually as possible:

'I'm a friend of Hal Jordan's.'

The reaction was noticeable and instantaneous. Whoever Jordan was, Brackett thought, he was nobody's lackey.

'What's your name?' the man asked.

'Brackett.'

'Never heard of you.'

'Jordan's heard of *you*,' Brackett replied and turned towards the door.

'Now wait a minute.'

Brackett felt a hand on his arm.

'Just wait a minute.'

He glanced back and saw the man, saw Taurus, shift his eyes quickly round the darkness and then say quietly, almost intimately:

'You replacing Loomis?'

'You heard about that?' Brackett said.

'Who hasn't? It's public knowledge.'

'Didn't see him last night, did you?'

The answer was obviously yes, but Taurus wasn't saying any more. He was unsure, giving Brackett the benefit of the doubt but that was all. He muttered something about attending to the bar, then hurried away, leaving Brackett alone, isolated in the chaos. He saw the man talking to a girl, then to a younger man who looked Cuban, saw him glance back, then they were all lost in the crowd. Colours changed from green to red to purple, a red-headed girl, with sequins on her cheeks that made her look sadly attractive, offered Brackett a drink, someone began to sing that he/she was Unwashed And Somewhat Slightly Dazed, and then Brackett saw him. He was black and he was fat, dressed like a lower-register piano player, stepping over legs and cushions and moving towards a door in the corner.

'Isn't that Murray?' Brackett said, and the redhead nodded.

Brackett saw the corner door open, noticed by the light that it was some form of toilet, waited for a full minute after it had closed, then followed. No one stopped him, no one asked him any more questions. They just receded around him like a channel tide as he opened the door, entered and locked it.

It was a small washroom, insanitary by any standards, broken tiles and graffiti, littered with tin-foil wrappers. A sink the colour of gravy, an empty condom machine (*Buy Me and Stop One*) and a single cubicle where the only other occupant of the room now sat, his feet visible beneath the partition doors. Brackett hesitated for a moment, studied the door (thin ply, distorted hinges), then he hit it with his shoulder, heard it splinter, heard a startled *Hey!*, saw the Jamaican try to rise but Brackett's hand was pushing down on the head, his foot treading hard on the bridge of trousers spanning the ankles. The Jamaican began to struggle, shouting out that he was clean and Brackett told him that he wasn't a cop and pushed him down again on to the seat.

'What *are* you then?' the Jamaican screamed. 'Some fucking fag?'

'No, Murray. I'm a friend of *hers*.'

Brackett pushed the polaroid snapshot before the Jamaican's face and Murray stared at it, then up at Brackett, then didn't move. Brackett let him go and stood back, his shoes in water and soiled newspaper. A discarded nasal spray.

'You know her, don't you?' he said.

The Jamaican suddenly became conscious of the indignity of his position and nervously crossed his stomach with his hands.

'Be a good boy, Murray,' Brackett continued. 'And then I'll leave you alone.'

Murray closed his mouth tightly until Brackett replaced the photograph by a crisp twenty-dollar bill and pushed it neatly into the pocket of the Jamaican's shirt.

'Now then, Murray, let's begin again.'

The Jamaican stared at the money, then at Brackett and shook his head.

'For twenty dollars, I don't know nothing. I don't even know the time.'

Brackett moved closer to him. The Jamaican flinched but that was all.

'Murray,' Brackett said wearily, 'the door behind me is locked. There's just you and I in here. No one else. Now think about that.'

Murray thought about it for fifty seconds. He probably even

wondered whether Brackett was carrying a gun, but even if he wasn't he knew that he didn't exactly have the advantage. He also knew that he had very little to sell, for no one at any level would tell him anything. At best, he was an amateur pusher, selling Turkey packets of coke to college boys and kindergarten socialites who might just as well have bought talcum powder. And at worst, he was a nuisance, a grub under a Cuban heel, a fat, hideous bird picking at the teeth of an alligator that could eat him. And probably would. He was in no position to bargain with anyone, including the family grocer, especially sitting with his trousers down before someone like Brackett who could well be as indifferent to his life as the Jamaican was to others. Common sense, therefore, prevailed, after the initial genuflection to his pride.

'Are you sure you're not a narc?'

'If it makes it easier,' Brackett said, 'I could be.'

Murray studied Brackett then pushed the side of his nose with his thumb.

'No. You're not a narc. They *take*. They don't give.'

'Anyone particular in mind?'

'On the take? Are you kidding me?'

The Jamaican laughed as if Brackett had asked him if the world was round.

'Jordan?' Brackett asked casually.

'A river in the Bible,' Murray said without batting an eyelid. 'Do I get to shoot for forty?'

Brackett smiled. He liked the tactics.

'Look,' Murray said, 'do you mind if I put my pants on?'

'No. You're fine as you are. Just tell me about the girl.'

'Shit, man, I can't talk like this –'

'The girl, Murray.'

The Jamaican sighed:

'I know nothing about her. She's just some chick who used to come in here.'

'Like last night?'

'Last night?'

'About four o'clock.'

'Oh yeh. But she was only here a few minutes.'

'Did you see her leave?'

'Sure. I was out in the street. Is this what the twenty bucks is for?'

'Mostly.'

Murray looked at Brackett in amazement, then shrugged:

'I thought – aw, hell, man, can't I put my pants on now?'

'Murray,' Brackett said. 'Everybody out there knows we're in here. Now they may think of a hundred reasons why the door's locked, but sooner or later, and probably sooner, someone's going to try and get in. So just answer the questions.'

'You English? Ever been to Kingston?'

Brackett sighed and reached for the twenty-dollar bill.

'All right, all right,' Murray said quickly, stopping the hand. 'What do you want to know? Jesus, it stinks in here.'

'She was with someone when she left here, wasn't she?'

'The chick? Yeh. Loomis. Say – did you hear about him?'

'Keep it in mind and tell me what happened when they left here.'

'They *left*. What else?'

'How?'

'How? By car.'

'A yellow car? Japanese?'

'Japanese? Who knows? A big fucking mother.'

'And Loomis got in the car as well?'

'Sure. He got in the car. I saw him. Got right in the car. Sat in the back. I was standing right there.'

'Doing what?'

'Me? A little of this. A little of that.'

'And the girl?' Brackett asked. 'She drove?'

'Yeh.'

'While Loomis sat in the back. Don't you think that odd?'

The Jamaican pursed his lips, then shrugged:

'No. Maybe he just wanted to sit next to the other guy.'

'The *other* guy?' Brackett asked bewildered. 'What other guy?'

Murray had now stood up and was pulling up his pants.

'I don't know. He was sitting in the back.'

'Did you know him?'

'No. I couldn't even see him too well. I mean it was dark and that.'

'But he was there? The other man?'

'Oh yeh. He was there. When the girl opened the door, the light went on. He switched it off fast, but I saw him.'

'What did he look like?'

'I don't know. It was too fast. White...'

Brackett studied the Jamaican for a moment, then:

'Where was he sitting?'

'In the back. I told you.'

'But where? Behind the girl –'

'Behind her. I remember Loomis had to walk round the car.'

'And then she drove the car away.'

'Yeh.'

'Thanks.'

Brackett walked to the door.

'Is that all?' Murray called after him, standing in the wreck of the cubicle.

'That's all.'

'Well, shit, man – next time you want something, don't come at me like you did. I thought it was a fucking ripoff.'

'Count yourself lucky.'

Brackett tried to smile but he couldn't. He simply unlocked the door and returned to the inferno. There was, at the time, nothing more to say. Nothing more could surprise him. Until he realized that all these events, since that first visit to the morgue, had taken place in no more than thirteen hours.

The weekend had hardly just begun.

The boy waited in the shadows of the hall until the sound of traffic had died away, then he cautiously opened the front door and glanced up and down the street. Nothing was in sight. Slowly he counted to twenty, breathed deeply, tucked the canvas bag under his jacket, then ran, ran as fast as he could, avoiding the street lights, ran through the darkness and didn't ease up until he had covered six blocks.

Brackett thought about Horowitz. Standing once again in the main room of Jimi's, conscious of the atmosphere and the scrutiny, he realized that the last thing he wanted now was for Sidney Horowitz to enter, show a badge to Taurus, walk over to him and say Hallo. That wouldn't do at all. Not that he intended joining the club (Brackett didn't join anything and that was that), but simply because he wanted to preserve whatever cover he had. It was, he realized, as transparent as cellophane, but it offered some protection and who knew when he might need it again. He could see the Cuban studying him (oiled hair, Gable moustache, a diamond or two), presented him with a smile to keep him guessing, then turned to the redhead:

'Where's the phone?' Brackett asked.

'The phone?'

'Yes. The phone. You got a phone?'

'Sure.'

'So where is it?'

'Through there.'

'Show me.'

'It's just through the door.'

'So show me through the door.'

The redhead looked at him, pouted, then took his arm.

'What's your name?' she said.

'What?'

'Let me guess. Charles? Like the prince.'

The Cuban was now making a detour through the darkness, circling the room towards the toilet.

'Look, sweetheart –' Brackett began.

'Sweetheart?' the redhead said with a smile. 'Nobody ever called me *that* before.'

'Just show me the phone.'

'You call everybody "sweetheart"?'

'I go easy on cab-drivers. Show me the phone.'

'Philip? Is that warm?'

Brackett sighed, removed her arm and walked towards the main door. Somebody entered, but it wasn't Horowitz.

'My name's Zelda.'

The redhead had taken his arm again.

'That's not my real name.'

'You surprise me,' Brackett said. He was now through the door.

'I read this book about this girl called Zelda,' the redhead continued. 'Well, I didn't read all of it. But I liked her name. Don't you like the name?'

'I can't see the phone. Where's the phone?'

'She was married to this writer. Hemingway. You ever read Hemingway?'

'Look –'

'Zelda. With a zee.'

'I thought you said there was a phone here?'

'Going to call up a girl?'

They had turned the corner of the corridor when Brackett saw it. It was a sedan chair, or at least it had been. But now, as if to add some semblance of imagination, it had been painted pink and converted into a phone-booth and placed away from the noise. Brackett removed the redhead's arm again.

'Thanks,' he said as pleasantly as possible. 'I'll take it on my own from here.'

'Do you want me to sit inside with you?'

'No. I'll manage. Why don't you wait for me back in the club?'

Another pout. Eyes mis-focusing for a moment.

'You going to come back?'

'After I've made the call.'

'You won't be long?'

'No.'

'I'll wait by the door.'

'Fine.'

Brackett stared at her, one hand on the top of the sedan chair until the redhead reluctantly took the hint and walked a few steps along the corridor, then stopped, looking back at him like an anxious puppy.

'I could wait here. Just in case you get a busy signal.'

Brackett shook his head.

'Just give me a few minutes. Set me up a drink.'

The redhead hesitated, bit her lip, then said finally:

'Okay.'

After Brackett saw her reach the corner, he lowered his head to enter the sedan chair.

'Bet you forgot my name.'

She was still there.

'Zelda!' Brackett snapped. 'Now will you leave me alone?' Then, noticing her expression, tempered his tone: 'Just for a couple of minutes. All right?'

'Sorry,' the redhead replied. She considered a look of injured innocence, thought better about it and settled for another old stand-by. 'I'm sorry. I was being . . . possessive. I know men don't like women to be, well, you know. . .'

'Possessive.'

'Yes.'

'So I'll see you in the club.'

'Zelda.'

'Zelda.'

'With a zee.'

She made a visual *Z* with her index finger, then smiled and walked away. Brackett heard a sudden fanfair of music as a door opened then closed. He entered the sedan chair, sitting on a padded seat, and put a coin in the pay-phone. Instinctively he was going to call Horowitz at home, then remembered that Sidney was on duty as he was dialling, and put down the receiver. He was about to dial again, when instead the phone suddenly rang, the noise echoing in the confined space of the wooden booth. Brackett stared at it, startled at first, then was puzzled and eventually curious. He picked it up and listened and a girl's voice said:

'Hallo?'

It was Zelda.

'I forgot to ask what you wanted to drink.'

Brackett swore, then out of habit inherited with his passport, he apologized.

'I didn't mean that.'

'That's okay. So what'll it be? An Old-Fashioned?'

'Zelda – I'm trying to make a call.'

But she wasn't listening. She was taking his order, reciting like a child the whole gallimaufry of cocktails, the nursery rhyme of Manhattans and You're Welcomes and Whiskey Sours that constituted the American diet. Brackett tried to interrupt, wondering why he couldn't hear any music counterpointing her voice, and then suddenly he began to move.

It was imperceptible at first, a rising and sinking, as if he were on a boat dictated by the waves. But he wasn't on a boat and this wasn't a cabin. It was a telephone booth, despite its appearance, and he was being lifted up. Someone, or more precisely two people, had picked up the handles of the sedan chair and were raising it like Regency flunkies. Brackett tried to turn, tried to see what was happening, his hand still holding the phone ('What about Planter's Punch? That's with rum. Or maybe a Daiquiri?'), then the horizon tilted sharply and the booth was smashed hard against the wall. He began to struggle, reaching for the door, but he was being tilted backward, and the booth hit the wall again, throwing him sideways. He couldn't move; he was trapped, thrown around – there must be at least four of them now – and then he caught a glimpse of Murray's face grinning at him, heard the recipe for a Margarita before he was pitched backwards, his head striking the wooden frame, and the phone was stretched and ripped from its moorings. He grappled again for the door but he was now on his side. He could see the ceiling as the booth smashed to the floor again, was carried, scraped across concrete, spun round, and he saw the stairs. A flight of stairs descending into the darkness below.

Brackett twisted round, braced himself with his feet, but it was too late. His head snapped back and he was upside down as the sedan chair tilted on the top stair, hesitated, a thrust, and it slowly toppled over and dropped. There was nothing he could do. Blurred images, a hovering in mid-air, panic as he covered his head with his arms and then the crash, smashing his breath from his body, tumbling downwards. He heard wood splintering as the box bounced from step to step, overturned, almost halted on the first flight but the momentum was too strong. It keeled over and pitched forward once more and Brackett cursed himself for being such a fool. There was a split second of almost blissful weightlessness, the zero G of a capsule in mid-air, and then it fell, plunged downwards, overturned, and the sound of feminine laughter was heard from above.

Sunday

11

'Walter?'

The shoes were expensive, the Italian kind that have to be cleaned with a neutral polish. If one ever buys them, the salesman presents them to the customer in individual woollen bags with a drawstring on top and sometimes throws in a pair of shoe trees as well.

'Walter – are you all right?'

The shoes were now replaced by a face looking directly at Brackett with that expression of intense concern adopted by those celebrities who interrupt the Saturday cartoons to tell the kiddies how charitable they are. Brackett didn't reply because he was wondering why he was lying on a stone floor, surrounded by a gawping crowd and holding a telephone receiver in his hand.

'Look, Walter, we'd better get out of here,' the face said. 'Can you move?'

Brackett slowly raised his head and looked up at Horowitz, was about to reply when he remembered what had happened and passed out.

It was dark outside and the fascia clock read one twenty-five. Brackett was sitting in the front seat next to Horowitz as they drove back across the town. He hadn't said anything for ten minutes since he had woken up to find himself in Horowitz's estate car (Horowitz being fond of both children and hunting), and realized that his body was all in one piece.

He had also been silent because he had been trying to concentrate, attempting to reassemble the jumble of facts, the 'relevant data' of the past day. It wasn't easy at the best of times, but he appreciated his friend's concern as he told him that he was all right and then told him again and then listened to a monologue that seemed oddly nervous, as if it had been Horowitz who had been bounced down the stairs and not himself.

'Sidney,' Brackett said at last, 'do me a favour and keep your eyes on the road.'

'I'm sorry, Walter,' Horowitz replied. 'I'm just worried about you, that's all.'

'So stop worrying.'

'I'm just glad you told me where you would be. I can't think what might have happened if I hadn't known.'

'But you did and I'm grateful.'

They were both quiet for a moment, both still thinking of the incident at Jimi's. Finally Brackett looked across at Horowitz and said:

'Sidney?'

'Yes?'

'You haven't told me what happened to you.'

'What do you mean – what happened to me?'

'About the girl. You said Homicide had something new on the girl.'

Horowitz glanced quickly across at Brackett:

'Let it wait till morning, Walter. You're in no shape –'

'Sidney – what happened?'

A pause. Horowitz turned in profile, neon lights highlighting his features, then he checked the rear-view mirror and brought the car to a halt at the kerb. He switched off the engine and stared for a moment at the street. Brackett waited.

'Walter . . .' Horowitz began then stopped.

Brackett sighed.

'Sidney, don't hold out on me. It isn't my fault I got involved in this, and Jesus Christ I don't even know why I am.'

'It's classified, Walter –'

'Oh come on, Sidney. You're going to tell me anyway.'

Horowitz shrugged. A shy grin.

'Sidney,' Brackett said quietly, leaning towards him. 'Will it help if I tell you something first? Like we're exchanging notes? For example, the girl wasn't alone in the car.'

Horowitz stared at him, startled:

'How did you learn –'

'Am I right?'

'Yes, but –'

'So what did Homicide tell you?'

'It wasn't an accident.'

'What wasn't?' Brackett asked.

'The girl's death. It wasn't an accident.'

Brackett stared blankly at Horowitz. Outside a man and woman walked by unsteadily, the woman laughing. The man banged on the roof, shouted something and walked on.

'Son of a bitch,' Horowitz said.

'Sidney – what do you mean, it wasn't an accident?'

'Simmons. . .'

'What about Simmons?'

'He asked for another check on the body and they found bruises on the girl's neck that were obviously the result of strangulation. Attempted or otherwise. She was probably dead before she went through the windscreen. That's what the report thinks. I mean it was a hundred to one chance that we found out. Simmons just wanted to double-check everything connected with Loomis and the girl happened to be one of them. So now it's murder.'

'What a day,' Brackett said. 'What a fucking day.'

'In a moving car. The bastard took a risk.'

Brackett didn't reply.

'You know,' Horowitz said, almost with regret, 'it could have been perfect.'

Brackett stubbed in the automatic car lighter and put a cigarette in his mouth.

'Does Simmons know who did it?' he said after a moment.

'No. He thinks it's Loomis.'

Brackett shook his head and stared at the red glow of the lighter.

'The girl was strangled from behind, wasn't she?'

'How did you know that?'

'She *was*, wasn't she?'

'How the hell did you know that?'

'Give me credit, Sidney. Was she?'

'Yes.'

'Loomis was in the car but he didn't murder the girl. Someone else did. Someone sitting right behind her as she drove. Right there.'

Horowitz stared at Brackett, a look of confusion in his eyes.

He watched as Brackett lit the cigarette then leant back in the seat.

'You sure been busy today, Walter. Haven't you?'

'Uh huh,' Brackett said and repeated, pointing, 'right there. Someone saw all three of them last night as they left Jimi's.'

'Who?'

'It doesn't matter who.'

'Well, he must have a name –'

'Listen, Sidney, let me tell you what I think. The girl – you don't know who she is yet, do you?'

'No.'

'No one even reported her missing?'

'No –'

'Jesus Christ...' A pause, then: 'Well, anyway, the girl borrowed a client's car. The Toyota. She went to Jimi's because she wanted some money, and there she meets Loomis. All fact.'

'Who told you?'

'Wait. Wanted some money. She gets in the car, behind the wheel. In the back, two men. Two. Loomis and another. She's scared. Knows who the other man is but doesn't know he's in the Toyota till it's too late. He tells her to drive. So she does. She's stoned and she's scared. They cross the town, past Union Square, past the palm trees, to the Bridge. On the bridge, the man behind her – not Loomis but the man directly behind the girl – strangles her. Car crashes, but by that time both men are out of the car. Now, think on this, Sidney. Loomis has seen it. He didn't know what was going to happen, but now he's seen it. And he's a witness. So he runs. Why? Because he knows, he fucking *knows* he's going to be killed too. So he runs straight to the police. They're at the toll-booth. Runs there because that's the safest place he can be. He's protected.'

Brackett stopped, folded his arms and looked at Horowitz. Horowitz blinked.

'So why doesn't he tell the truth? About the other man?'

'Maybe he's going to,' Brackett said, leaning forward, speaking quickly. 'But don't forget Loomis is implicated. He's almost an accomplice. He even *works* for the other man. Whatever he says he's going to involve himself, so he makes up a story, marking time. And what happens? The police believe it. They damn well believe it. Why shouldn't they? Accidents happen all the time.'

'So he's off the hook.'

'No, Sidney. He's not. Not to the other man. *He*'s not safe until Loomis is dead. Because Loomis was going to talk. Not to the police. But to me.'

'Why you?'

'I don't know,' Brackett said. 'I never had time to find out.'

Horowitz began to drum his hands on the steering wheel, then lit a cigarette and stared pensively at the darkness.

'It's guesswork, isn't it, Walter? That's all it is. I mean, this other man –'

'He exists. He calls himself Jordan. Hal Jordan.'

'Billy Kent tell you that?'

'Yes. I tell you, Sidney, tomorrow I'm going to take another look at that Toyota.'

Horowitz didn't say a word. He looked worried and Brackett sensed it.

'Don't you believe me, Sidney?' Brackett asked.

'I don't know, Walter. I think somehow you should leave this to the police.'

'Sidney –' Brackett protested.

'Well, look what happened to you. You could have been killed back there.'

'I can take care of myself. Besides, I don't think that was anything to do with Jordan. If he'd wanted to kill me, he would have done. I think that was just some goofheads getting a bit uptight.'

'Maybe so, but I'm just saying –'

'Sidney, you of all people –'

'I just think that you shouldn't –'

'What?'

'Will you listen to me!'

'Not if you fucking shout,' Brackett said, suddenly angry. 'For Christ's sake, I'm not going to give up now. I'm that close to it. *That* close.'

Brackett glared at Horowitz then looked away and stared fixedly out of the window. There was a long pause. A man crossed the street in front of them carrying a pile of newspapers, turned his head as an ambulance was heard in the distance, then continued, reading headlines as he walked away.

'I'm sorry, Walter,' Horowitz said quietly. 'I didn't mean... Well, I was just thinking of what happened to Harry.'

Brackett was listening but he made no reaction.

'I mean, Harry knew everyone,' Horowitz continued. 'He had everything. Knew all the contacts. Walter, he was the best and we both know it. Then look what happened. A couple of kids, no more than kids, almost kick him to death. For what?'

'Harry knew what he was doing.'

'Sure. He was stubborn. Like you.'

'Yes,' Brackett said emphatically. 'Like me.'

Horowitz studied him for a moment, then seemed to retreat to the far corner of the car.

'Sidney,' Brackett said, leaning close to him. 'You're the only one I can talk to. You must understand what this means to me.'

'You would never have said that twenty years ago.'

Brackett smiled:

'Twenty years ago I would have run a mile from this. Murder was never my line. That was Harry's department. But now I need this. If I blow it, then that's it.'

'And so you listen to punks like Billy Kent?'

'Yes. And others. Anyone.'

'At Jimi's?'

'Why not?'

'No one's going to go into court for you from there.'

'I don't expect them to. But I've learnt some things.'

'What?'

Brackett shrugged:

'Things...'

'Walter, you're talking to a friend.'

'I know that. And you've been a good friend. I remember when Dorothy died...'

'No hearts and flowers.'

'I'm not giving you hearts and flowers,' Brackett said. 'I'm telling you. We're friends, but inside one of the pockets of your suit is a badge.'

'So?'

'So that's all.'

'Are you telling me you can't speak to me because of the badge?'

'In this case, yes.'

Horowitz stared at him, then said:

'You're crazy, Walter. I really believe you're insane.'

Brackett didn't smile.

'Take me home, Sidney,' he said. 'Start the car.'

There was a beat, then Brackett leant over and turned on the ignition. The engine hesitated and died.

'Put your foot on the gas, Sidney.'

Horowitz remained motionless for a moment, then started the car again. There was a sudden crescendo of noise, six cylinders moving, and the estate wagon eased away from the kerb.

They drove for about four blocks in silence, and then Horowitz said as they rested at a light:

'You know, Walter, I don't know a damn thing that's in your mind.'

'That's how I want it to be,' Brackett replied. 'I don't want to make any mistakes until I'm sure.'

'Sure of what?'

Brackett was about to reply. He had known Sidney Horowitz for too long to behave the way he did. He hated that in other people; hated those poker-table bluffs, the deceits. He wanted to speak openly, say he was looking for a cop, one of the fuzz, one of Frisco's finest who wasn't so fine any more. He wanted to put his cards on the table because he owed it to the man next to him more than anyone else apart from Kemble. It was Horowitz who had nursed him through the worst times, the petty sloughs of despondency that had dictated his life for the past ten years. Sidney. The friend who had invited him to his house so many times, made him a guest, given him a godson. Sidney Horowitz who had the jokes, who lent him money when the rent was overdue and who phoned him on Sundays to take him to the ballgame. Remember that? Nostalgia is all the rage. But Brackett couldn't speak. *Time you took stock of your life, Walter.* That's what it was. An empty filing cabinet for the past decade, because he had drunk too much, pitied himself too much and achieved nothing. He had failed. *Was* a failure, and Simmons had demonstrated that.

Oh, at first, it was easy to dismiss Kemble as being the bulwark of his profession. But he was. It didn't need a computer to decipher that. Today, yesterday, the last fourteen hours, he was in reach of proving his own – what is it? – status. Ah, the Americans love that. Status. Bugger them all. But it was true. The status. Rank. Mr Walter Brackett – haven't you heard? He couldn't afford the mistakes. He had to be sure. Certain. It had to be Brackett's success. His and his alone. Fifty-three years old, Walter, and what have you got? Sounds like a song. Jesus fucking Christ. Do I suspect everyone? The drunk on the corner. Charlie sitting in his fat limousine (fifty dollars from the airport? Music extra?). The owner of the drug store? Liebermann. Harry. Bouncing. That's what it was. Bouncing down those stairs. The bastards. No one's going to do that to *me*! I've got files. I've written it all down. There. Longhand. Jesus Christ. The lights turned green. Jesus fucking Christ. Oh, Sidney – is it you? Jordan. Hal Jordan. That poor girl. Oh, please don't go round Union Square, baby. I hate those palm trees. *Every*one. Everyone's guilty. Simmons said that. Everyone. Got to listen to Simmons. Clever bastard. Motherfucker. That's what the Yanks say. Them with their chocolate and gum. Where were you in 1940 when the bombs destroyed – destroyed, annihilated the house? Who made *you* an orphan? Damn you all. Pearl Harbor! Was that petty – ah, yes, petty, Petty Calendar – petty incident the starting gate for your war? Two years, buster. Two fucking years we fought before you appeared. Oh yes. So you want me to take it? Accept it? Lights turned green and red again, why doesn't Sidney move? Now he moves. *Now* he decides to move. Oh yes. Well this time, I, *I* don't need you. On my own. Over the hill. Not over the hill. Over the *top*. Top! Fucking crooked cops. That girl. So young, the wisp of hair, playing hookey from us all. I'll tell Horowitz. I'll tell him. Just you watch. I'll tell that –

'Sidney!'

The scream hit the air at the same time as Horowitz slammed on the brakes. The car immediately slithered sideways, the tyres grasping for a hold on the wet surface as Brackett struggled for the door, grappled to open the door, and then snapped, his face pressed against the window, his voice rising once more to a scream, snapped as neatly as the breaking of a breadstick.

Brackett stared at the sink, at the water slowly orbiting the plug. He watched the water rise, and decided not to move until it had covered at least two links of the chain.

'How are you feeling now, Walter?'

Who was that? Who was that standing behind him? Brackett turned his head, almost collapsed, and seized the edge of the porcelain, and gazed up at the light over his head, counted the pupil of dead flies in the centre of the bowl, then frowned, not recognizing the wallpaper or the towels or the framed caricatures on one wall.

'You really cracked up back there,' Horowitz said, and a hand appeared holding a cold flannel. 'At one point I had to strap you to the seat, otherwise I don't know what you would have done. Believe me, Walter, you really cracked up!'

Warily, nervously, as if terrified to disturb the very air around him, Brackett raised his head, puzzled why everything seemed to stretch above him, towering like skyscrapers, and saw Horowitz receding towards the ceiling; he saw the belt buckle, the gun in the holster, the loose threads on the tie, the glass of whiskey reflecting promenades of light, the chin, a smell of sweat, and then that smile, that pulpit smile of beneficence, that Revell-kit smile that said, 'All better now'.

'What am I doing here?' Brackett said as the smile descended, performed an impromptu repertoire of grimaces, scowls, beams behind the shimmering liquid in the glass, and then it opened, revealing an encore of teeth, and said:

'Drink up, Walter. Miriam's making us some soup.'

It was leek and potato because Miriam was under the misconception that it was Brackett's favourite. She stood, hair in rollers, arms folded, a ladle ready in her hand, watching Brackett eat.

'Good?' she asked, an expression of concern, her eyes never leaving the soup.

Brackett swallowed, timed his answer as if he were tasting a rare Mouton-Rothschild, and then said:

'Good.'

Miriam smiled and pushed the tureen into a more conspicuous position on the table. Brackett stared at it as it now upstaged Horowitz sitting opposite him.

'I still think you ought to stay the night here,' Horowitz said. 'We could make up a bed in the spare room.'

Brackett shook his head.

'Thanks, Sidney, but I'm fine now. I've troubled you enough.'

'No trouble. Tell him, Miriam.'

'It's no trouble, Walter. When else do we get a chance to see you?'

'It's the middle of the night, Miriam,' Brackett said. 'I'd rather get home. No offence.'

Miriam glanced at her husband, who pulled a face of 'what can *I* do?', then gestured to her to leave the room. Miriam hesitated, then ladled some more soup into Brackett's plate.

'Eat up, Walter. It's all yours.'

Brackett swallowed again and managed a smile. Another gesture from Horowitz, head tilted towards the door, and Miriam reluctantly left, returned almost immediately with a plate of cold meat and pickles, retreated once more and was heard washing dishes in the kitchen.

'Miriam, why don't you go to bed?' Horowitz called out from the door, raised his eyes to the ceiling, then turned his attention back to Brackett.

'Boy,' he said, 'you *really* cracked up back there. You really hit the roof.'

Brackett stared at the soup.

'I'm sorry about that, Sidney. Delayed reaction.'

'Oh, sure. Don't worry about it. But, Walter, you really cracked up. Pow!'

'Sidney?'

'Yes?'

'Do you mind if I . . . ?'

Brackett pointed to the soup.

'What? Oh no. Leave it. Leave it. Let the kids suffer tomorrow. I tell you, I'm married to the only Jewish momma who can't cook.'

There was a silence and Brackett studied the room. On a far wall was the traditional gallery of photographs, mostly of children playing on a beach, standing self-consciously in Disneyland, or riding a new bike. Brackett stood up and stared at them.

'They're growing up,' he said.

'Every day. The one who wants to be Namath is your godson.'

'No kidding?'

'Would you believe it? He's *nine*.'

'Mike's nine? Jesus ... where did the years *go*?'

Brackett stared at the photograph of a dark-haired boy holding a football and wearing a shirt emblazoned with the word *Jets*.

'He's got your nose, Sidney,' Brackett said and grinned. Horowitz smiled, rubbed his nose, and then said:

'Are you sure you're all right, Walter?'

'Don't keep saying that. I'm fine.'

Then, changing the subject, moved along the wall and found himself staring at a picture of himself. It had been taken eighteen years ago. He was standing on the steps of a small church and wearing a best suit with a carnation in his buttonhole. Holding his arm was Dorothy, and on his right, Kemble. In the background could be seen the face of Horowitz. Brackett stared at it then quickly shuffled his gaze to another photograph and said:

'Hey, is that you?'

It was a group photograph of police cadets posed before the austere gates of an academy.

'Of course it's me,' Horowitz said. 'Haven't you seen it before?'

'I must have. And that's Herb. Herb Johanssen.'

'Rookies together.'

'I thought –' Brackett began, then stopped.

'You thought he was older?' Horowitz said. 'No, Walter. Herb's just more ambitious. I guess he always had what it takes.

If you look closely, you'll see Simmons there too. That's the way it goes...'

Brackett was silent until Horowitz took his arm.

'Let me show you Mike.'

'What?'

'Mike. Your godson. Don't you want to see him?'

'Now?'

'Sure. Come on.'

Reluctantly, Brackett followed Horowitz into a small darkened bedroom, walking on tiptoes, and then stood piously staring down at a boy asleep in a bed.

'That's Mike,' Horowitz whispered proudly. 'Quite something, isn't he?'

Brackett nodded and studied the bed, then the posters on the walls, the plastic models, a shelf of toys, another shelf of books, football pennants. A pile of comics stacked on a table, mostly, as Brackett noticed, *Green Lantern* and *Tarzan*. A framed picture of Joe Namath. More toys and boxes of games. A half-assembled train set.

'Jesus, Sidney,' Brackett said, then immediately dropped his voice. 'What did you do? Buy out Schwarz?'

Horowitz almost blushed and replied: 'Can't give kids too much, you know, Walter? Life's such a stinking, rotten mess that kids deserve everything they can get. If I had to sell my house to stop Mike or Louise ending up like that girl at the morgue, I'd do it. No matter what I myself might do. That girl, Jesus, Walter, she's better off dead. She really is.'

'That's what Billy Kent said.'

'He's right.'

Brackett looked away embarrassed and idly picked up a comic. And then Horowitz said:

'Walter – I had to tell Simmons.'

Brackett turned and stared at him:

'What?'

'I'm sorry but I had to tell him. I'm supposed to be on duty now and...'

'What did you tell him?'

'Nothing much. Just about Loomis being in the Toyota, that's all. I had to. It's our case, not yours.'

The boy in the bed began to stir. Both men stared at him but the boy simply sighed in his sleep and turned on to his stomach.

'Let's go into the other room,' Horowitz whispered, and both men returned to the dining-room. Brackett glanced at the photographs again, not saying a word.

'I had to report in something,' Horowitz said apologetically.

'Why?' Brackett said, surprised by the strength of his voice. 'Why that? Wasn't the accident at Jimi's enough? It's not only *your* case, Sidney, it's mine too. So stop looking for kudos.'

'I'm not –'

'Well, then –'

'Well what?'

'Just well then. That's all.'

Horowitz glanced towards the kitchen, then said, quietly:

'I'm sorry, Walter. It's just that Simmons had been screaming for me for an hour and ... Well, I didn't want to get you into trouble. I mean that.'

Brackett was silent for a moment, then said:

'I understand, Sidney. I shouldn't have – I understand.'

Horowitz didn't move, while Brackett remained staring at the faces on the wall, the posed photographs; and then, inexplicably, he shuddered, almost as if he was suddenly aware, had suddenly been granted some bizarre sixth sense informing him that one of the faces before him was Jordan himself. Brackett tried to dismiss this, telling himself that he didn't believe in such things; that intuitions were deceptive, that he was tired, his mind shaken. But nevertheless, he couldn't deny that the emotion, the sensation had happened, valid or not. And worse, much worse, he also couldn't deny that it hadn't taken him by surprise. It wasn't sixth sense at all. To Brackett, it was cold sober realization.

'Take a seat, Walter, and let's calm down,' Horowitz said. 'I'll ask Miriam to make some coffee.'

Brackett didn't answer but walked to the door, avoiding Horowitz's eye, said:

'Goodnight, Sidney.'

And walked quickly to the top of the stairs.

He heard Horowitz call after him and saw a light go on, but Brackett was already in the hall. He glanced up, saw Horowitz gaping at him, saw Miriam appearing behind him, a percolator in one hand, then Brackett slammed the front door, banishing them from his sight, and hurried out into the comfort of the night air.

12

Out of necessity, Brackett tipped the cab driver the minimum and entered Fatty's delicatessen by the side door, treading carefully on the edges of the stairs for fear of waking the Liebermanns until he reached his office. As he opened the door and switched on the light, the girl smiled at him from across the room, like an ambitious chorine waiting naked by the casting couch for Mr Zee. Rejection was immediate as Brackett, his mind jumping shadows, unpinned the photograph and watched as the girl slumped to the floor, stretched her legs and then curled up into the corner and out of sight.

After checking the room and finding it undisturbed, he instinctively looked under the ashtray and discovered that there had been another two calls. One inevitably once more from Mrs Markstein, and the other, according to Liebermann, from a man who did not give his name. Brackett speculated on who that might be, found the list infinite as well as distracting, and consequently abandoned the pursuit.

It had been an exhausting and disturbing day by any standard, and too much of it had been dictated by other people and alien events. At this stage, Brackett wanted only to think, to try and graph the experiences and his analysis of those experiences into a recognizable and simple pattern, a guideline that he could consider and digest before moving on.

He therefore undressed, saw with relief that there were only a few bruises on his body, and covered them with a pair of blue-and-white cotton pyjamas, neatly patched and ironed by Mrs Liebermann. Finally, after collecting the Loomis file, a pen, some cigarettes, an ashtray, he got carefully into bed, adjusted pillows and read what he had written the previous day. Some of it he crossed out and some of it he answered or confirmed, either conclusively with a full stop or cautiously with an interrogation mark. He was surprised how many pages he had already written and how many names had been added (Mary Malewski he still wrote as *Mary Malewski*, despite the alternatives, since it simplified matters); he was also disturbed at many of the suggestions that had come to mind, some of them within the past hour. Suggestions not about *why* events had happened (murder is murder no matter what the justification), but about who had caused them. The very fact that he had written names down (three) indicated that he suspected someone known to him, even before that moment in Horowitz's house, and God knows he wished he could make it otherwise.

Brackett put the pages aside. A page dropped to the floor, almost rattling as it touched the carpet, and he realized how silent the room was. Even the traffic outside seemed mute. A tapestry of shadows covered the far wall, overlapping on to curtains and then the desk itself, moving the longer he stared at it as if a Polonius was behind the arras; moving into faces as Brackett began to daydream, despite himself, until suddenly, quite clearly and distinctly, he heard the footsteps. There was no mistake about what they were. They were footsteps, made not by a clandestine intruder who sought stealth, but by someone who quite openly and casually was walking around in the room above his head.

At first Brackett thought it was Liebermann until he realized that not only were the sounds wrong (Liebermann's walk being dictated by an emphatic shuffle as against this almost brisk stride), but that the Hungarian would not be up there in the first place. As both he and Brackett knew, the room above had not been used for over half a decade, having been left untouched, except for superficial dusting once a week, since the day the tenant had moved out. For it belonged then, and still did, to Harry Kemble.

Brackett didn't move but listened until the footsteps stopped in the corner of the room just above his head. He stared at the ceiling, and in the silence he thought for a moment that he'd imagined it, that his preoccupation with the murders had distorted reality, but he knew he hadn't. He knew it as he put on a raincoat over his pyjamas and hesitated by the window, his right hand near the desk drawer. Slowly he allowed his fingers to open the drawer and touch the gun, and then the gun was in his hand and in his pocket and Brackett was at the door and moving into the darkness of the corridor.

Kemble's room was at the top of a single flight of stairs, and even before Brackett reached it he could see the light shining under the door. Whoever was inside was either arrogantly bold or behaving as if he belonged there. Oddly this last supposition disturbed Brackett most, not because he feared to see his partner at home again, but merely because of what it might imply. If asked, Brackett could not elaborate on that, nor indeed would he try. At the door he stopped, transferred the gun to his left-hand pocket and then slowly and quite calmly turned the handle and allowed the door to swing open. A rectangle of light (the corner of a bed, a row of paperbacks on a shelf) and Brackett was stepping into the room as the man was turning, turning without surprise as if his presence was the most natural thing in the world.

'Oh there you are,' he said before Brackett could speak. 'I was wondering when you might arrive.'

Brackett stopped, taken aback, for he hadn't expected this reception at all. Nor had he expected to encounter, out of all people, Lieutenant Simmons.

'I really do apologize, Brackett,' Simmons said, leaning against the desk, 'I honestly thought it was *your* room. Where you slept.'

The two men were now downstairs, standing in Brackett's office. All the lights were on and Brackett was beginning to show his irritation, resenting Simmons's manner and conscious of his own image, standing there in striped pyjamas.

'It isn't my room, and even if it was, you've got no right to break in there, no matter what time of day.'

'But I didn't break in, Brackett,' Simmons replied holding up a bunch of keys on the crook of his index finger. 'I used one of these. Besides, I called you earlier but, unhappily, you were out.'

'You might have called, but you left no name nor any intention of coming here.'

'Didn't I?' A slight elevation of the eyebrows. 'But I talked to someone. A foreigner like you.'

'Liebermann's Hungarian, if that's what you mean.'

'Hungarian? Ah yes. That odd mixture of v's and w's.'

A smile. Brackett became aware of the gun that was conspicuous in his coat pocket, but if Simmons had noticed he made no comment but idly studied the desk, picking up an ashtray and then placing it down in its exact position in the dust.

'Well, now you're here,' Brackett said, 'what do you want?'

'Then the room above must be Kemble's,' Simmons said, ignoring the question and gesturing vaguely towards the ceiling light.

'Yes –'

'Yes. You must be expecting him to return from ... what's that place? You did tell me. Autumn Pastures. No, Autumn Glades.'

'I never told you –'

'You didn't? Never mind.' And then. '*Are* you?'

'What?'

'Expecting Kemble to return?'

'One day. Look – why are you here? Can't this wait till morning?'

Simmons looked at Brackett with a stage-managed expression of rejection, like a favourite uncle finding the door slammed in his face.

'Brackett ... I just wanted to thank you.'

'What for?'

The question was cold and suspicious.

'For your help. I was told about your theories regarding the girl's car, and so I decided to have the car dusted for prints. The seats ...'

Brackett said nothing but waited.

'And do you know what we found?'

'Tell me.'

'Loomis was in the car all right. No question about that. But he wasn't sitting behind the girl.'

This was said matter-of-factly as if Simmons knew he was telling Brackett something he had already learnt. Nevertheless he added: 'You don't seem surprised?'

'I'm not,' Brackett said.

Simmons gave a token nod of appraisal:

'Then you've discovered about the other man?'

'Yes.'

'Know who he is?'

'No.'

'Nor do we. No prints except for a glove smear over, I repeat *over* a print by Loomis.'

'Did the girl's murderer wear gloves?' Brackett asked, and saw Simmons hesitate then flick his head round towards him.

'You *knew* that she was murdered?'

'Yes,' said Brackett, savouring the moment and lighting a cigarette.

'I underestimated you,' Simmons said, attempting to regain his advantage. 'But then you are a detective. It says so on the door. However, I told you to stay out of this case.'

'I did,' Brackett said. 'I was only involved with the girl. I couldn't know that they'd both overlap, could I?'

Simmons began to reply then decided against it and asked instead:

'How did you find out? About the girl?'

'I was told.'

'By whom?'

'Sidney Horowitz.'

'Oh yes. Sidney Horowitz. He's an old friend of yours, isn't he?'

'We've known each other for a few years.'

'A few years? Then he knows you well. Has he been here?'

'Often.'

Simmons nodded, pursed his lips, looked round the room then nodded again.

'I see...'

They talked for perhaps a further ten minutes. At least Simmons talked while Brackett replied in monosyllables, then finally evaded any discussion altogether. It was inevitable, in retrospect, since Brackett wondered why Simmons, with all the resources of the police, should need him at all. Of course, Brackett at first was flattered, but this very flattery instilled in him a natural possessiveness, a reassessment of his own worth and he didn't want to share it with anyone.

Simmons began to turn to the subject of Billy Kent. He had checked out his room, checked out the gym, but the boy had disappeared. Gone to earth. According to Dixie, he had borrowed fifty dollars and said he would call from New York sometime.

'Did you know that?' Simmons asked.

Brackett shook his head but said he wasn't surprised, then mentioned Billy Kent's belief that the possible murderer was a cop. He said this deliberately, irritated by Simmons's behaviour, but to his surprise Simmons's reaction was tempered, almost restrained.

'They all say that, Brackett. Every kid with a grudge wants to put the finger on us. "They've been framed. They've been beaten up. The stuff was planted." Every single day we hear it.'

'*I* don't,' Brackett said.

'So when was the last time you were involved in a murder case?'

Brackett shrugged:

'That isn't the point. Billy Kent had no reason to accuse anybody.'

'And you believe him?'

'I believe he thought –'

'Thought?'

'Yes. Thought.'

'And you accept that?'

'Yes, lieutenant, I do. He didn't think the man was a grape-picker or a ballet-dancer. He thought he was a cop. There must have been a reason.'

'Maybe he likes grape-pickers and ballet-dancers.'

'I'm just reporting what he said. That's all.'

'Then if he's such a material witness, why the hell did you let him go?'

Brackett glanced at Simmons then looked away.

'I didn't know at the time how – all right, lieutenant, I made a mistake. But where were *you*?'

Simmons didn't even blink but said quietly:

'Are you telling me, Brackett, that you think the murderer is a cop?'

A hesitation and Brackett finished off a whiskey and placed the glass on the table.

'I think,' he replied slowly, 'that Billy Kent believed that the man he saw with the girl *behaved* like one. That he was on the side of the law.'

'Like you?' Simmons said, keeping his gaze steady.

'All right. Yes. Like me.'

'Well, whoever he is, he's not on the side of the law now. And thanks to you, Brackett, our star witness is probably halfway to Nevada.'

'Listen, Simmons,' Brackett said angrily. 'Don't use *me* as a patsy. I'm on my own, while you've got half the damn police force working for you! If you want a witness, go find Norma Wheatley.'

'We did,' Simmons said. 'She's dead.'

Brackett stared at him then turned away:

'Jesus Christ, how did I get into this fucking mess?'

'Nobody asked you. You chose it. We do this every day of the year because we're paid to. What's *your* excuse?'

Simmons didn't wait for an answer but stood up and walked towards the filing cabinet. He didn't attempt to open any of the drawers but leant on it, running his hand over the metal top.

'I'm keeping you from your sleep, aren't I?' he said.

'It doesn't matter any more,' Brackett replied.

'Well ... let me now tell you why I came here. It'll only take a moment.'

'You've taken half an hour already.'

'A few minutes more then. If you don't mind.'

Brackett did mind but he was curious, and so sat behind the desk and poured a drink.

'It's about the girl. Whoever she is. Sergeant Henderson told me she came and saw you.'

'Yes.'

'When?'

'I don't know. Three months ago.'

'And you wrote down her address. In a file I believe?'

'Yes. I told Henderson that.'

'I know. But now that file is lost. Or is it missing?'

'Missing,' Brackett said.

'Someone took it?'

'So I believe.'

'Any other files missing?'

'Not as far as I know.'

Simmons began to tap on the cabinet with his fingers.

'So the person who took the file must have known it was here.'
'Obviously,' Brackett sighed.
'Did you tell anyone? About the girl coming here?'
'Henderson.'
'Before that?'
'No,' Brackett said. 'Only –'
He stopped. Simmons raised his head:
'Only who?'
'Only Kemble, but I tell him everything –'
'Why did you hesitate?' Simmons said pointedly.
'I didn't hesitate.'
'You hesitated, Brackett. Why?'
'Look,' Brackett said, his voice rising, 'There are dozens of people who have been in this room over the months. This is an office. It's open all day. It's obvious I'm going to keep records of clients.'
'Was the girl a client?'
'Not exactly.'
'Why "not exactly"?'
'She never returned. That's why. I took some notes. That's all. She could have stolen the damn thing herself.'
Simmons nodded.
'Yes, perhaps. But why should she?'
'I've no idea.'
'She'd have to get in here and out again without being seen.'
'Naturally –'
'But the only way in is through the delicatessen. At least during the day. She'd be seen there.'
'Yes –'
'Unless she came through the side door. But that would be impossible, wouldn't it?'
'*You* got in that way.'
'But you forget,' Simmons said, 'I have a key. A skeleton key but a key nevertheless.'
'That's not difficult to get.'
'You mean – if you're on the side of the law?'
'Or the opposite.'
Simmons glanced at Brackett.
'Well, whatever. At least we've established that whoever took

the file had to have a key. Of some kind. And I also think that the same person wanted the file because they were worried what the girl might have said. Which eliminates the girl.'

A beat. Then:

'What *did* she say, Brackett?'

'Nothing much.'

'She must have said *something.*'

'A sob story, that's all. She said her name was Mary Malewski, but it could have been any name.'

'Did you know that then?'

'No. Why should I? She said that was her name and I believed it.'

'You believe everything anyone tells you?'

'Yes. Sometimes. I'd never seen her before and she came in and said something about wanting to try and find her father. But what she wanted was money.'

'Which you gave her?'

'Yes...'

'Did you ask her why she wanted to find her father?'

'I didn't have a chance.'

'Why not?'

'Because,' Brackett said, 'she suddenly ... I don't know ... she just suddenly panicked and ran out.'

'Panicked?'

'Well ... maybe she just lost her nerve.'

Simmons studied Brackett, puzzled.

'When did she panic? Did you say anything to make her –'

'Not as far as I know. She seemed all right at first. I asked her a few things and she seemed relaxed. And then she sat down and I started writing and the next minute she was rushing out of the room.'

'Didn't you think that odd?'

'Sure. But I get freaks coming in here just like you do.'

'And that's all?'

'That's all. I assume that all she wanted was money. It was a hustle.'

'But why panic?'

Brackett shrugged. He had to admit that it had puzzled him as well, but then it didn't seem important. At least not as important as Simmons seemed to think. He watched him as the detective walked up and down the room, keeping his face in profile, then finally sat in the armchair and stared into space.

'Don't make yourself comfortable,' Brackett said. 'Because I'm going to throw you out now.'

Simmons looked up and was about to move when suddenly he stopped, his eyes focused on the wall behind the door.

'That's extraordinary,' he said.

'What?'

'You know, I never noticed those photos before.'

He was pointing to the two pictures framed on the wall.

'What about them?' Brackett asked.

'Nothing. It's just that it's the first time since I've been in this room that I've seen them. Strange isn't it?'

'I never thought about it.'

'Is the top one your wife?'

'Yes.'

'Divorced?'

'No.'

The tone of Brackett's voice said everything and Simmons made no comment.

'And the other is you and Kemble?'

'Yes.'

'Strange.'

'Why do you keep saying it's strange?'

'Nothing. This is the chair the girl sat in. Before she ran out.'

'Yes, but what does it matter which chair?'

Simmons didn't answer but instead stood up and walked to the door, said, 'Goodnight, Brackett,' and was gone without even looking back. His footsteps were heard descending the steps, a door was opened and closed and then nothing, except Brackett standing by the armchair motionless, staring not at the open door but towards the photos on the wall.

It was two more hours before he finally fell asleep, and only then after resorting to sleeping pills. When he awoke, his body was cold with sweat, a physical memento from his dreams. On his bedside table was a piece of paper on which he had written in the early hours the single word *Why?* The rest of the sheet was blank.

Brackett didn't even look at it but dressed in the same clothes he'd worn the previous day. He didn't shave, abandoning routine, abandoning everything, as he left the room, locked the door and went out into the grey light of Sunday morning. He avoided Liebermann because he didn't want to speak trivialities to anyone. He simply wanted to find a cab and pick up his car.

And then drive to Autumn Glades.

13

Four men were sitting under a rather disdainful fig-tree that looked as though it had realized long ago that this artificial landscape was not another Eden and never would be. The men were playing cards, a variation of poker, when Brackett approached them, walking along the shrub-lined path (hibiscus in evidence) from the cabanas.

He, Brackett, had taken his time driving from the city, deliberately taking the long route on the pretence that it was more scenic, that he would avoid the Sunday drivers, but he had to admit that twice he almost turned back.

Moreover, it had seemed strange (he might even use the word 'unnatural') to visit Kemble on a Sunday or indeed any day except Saturday, for he couldn't recall ever doing it before. He had been aware of church bells, of shops that were normally open being closed, of seeing people dressed in their best clothes. At one point he had stopped at a drugstore and bought some comics since he didn't want to arrive empty-handed. He had also bought a newspaper and had read the report on Loomis's murder. It was no more than half a column under two photos – one of Loomis himself (a mug shot taken from the police files), and one of Johanssen looking serious and 'in command' as if posing for a postage stamp. Nothing was said that Brackett didn't already know, apart from minor details about Loomis's criminal record, and a great deal was not said at all. Simmons was not mentioned, leaving all the speeches to Johanssen who played his part in true character, upstaging everyone. '*There's no question that the murderer is a psychopath*' and '*I am fully cognizant with the facts*' and '*The citizens of San Francisco can rest assured that I will make it my personal responsibility*' (Brackett liked that line. He could see Johanssen rehearsing it now), '*Yes we do have a clue to the murder.*' Really, Herb?

As expected no mention was made of Mary Malewski, at least as a murder victim, save for an unrelated paragraph on a middle page that reported the car crash. Simmons was obviously, for reasons of his own, presenting the charade that the police believed it to be simply an accident and nothing more.

The old man in the plaid jacket reshuffled the cards and looked up at Brackett.

'If you've got the money, pull up a chair.'

'No thanks,' Brackett said. 'I'm looking for a friend of mine. Harry Kemble.'

'Harry Kemble?'

'That's right.'

'Well, we don't see much of him lately. Try his room.'

'He's not there.'

All four men were now studying Brackett, assessing him with mild curiosity. Not one of them was under sixty years of age but that didn't seem to worry them. Nor, as Brackett observed by the money on the table, were they likely to be worried in the future. They resembled four elder senators, not from Washington but from Rome, sitting out their remaining years with smug apathy to anything that didn't belong in their narrow sphere.

'Then if he's not there,' a second man said, 'it's because it's Sunday.'

'Sunday?' Brackett said. 'What's that got to do with it?'

'You sure you're a friend of Harry Kemble's?'

'That's what I said.'

'Then you ought to know that on Sunday Harry will be found in there.'

The second man was pointing towards a building standing aloof from the cabanas and shaded by cypress trees.

'What is it?' Brackett asked.

'That,' said the dealer, integrating the cards under the arch of his hand, 'is the chapel.'

It was, in fact, more like a Big Top, a three-ring circus, than a chapel; not in the nature of its spectacle but in its design. It appeared to encompass at least ten denominations, from the primness of American Esoteric to the Roxy of Roman Catholicism. It entertained rabbi, priest and preacher on varying

Sabbaths and on varying floors, and celebrated those Holy Days that jostled most for attention; it was a market place for the agnostic and the tyro who could wander at will from room to room, sampling the rituals, checking the odds or rejecting them all. It was gaudy, of course, but no more than a World's Fair; and if its architecture was not as near to God as St Peter's or Westminster Abbey, its ageing congregation certainly were, give or take a year or two.

Brackett however found the building suffocating, reminding him of a city bank where everything was too large, too high and too cabalistic, inducing in him the feeling that no matter how rich he was, his credit was suspect. In that sense, perhaps, that emotion was appropriate for a church as well, but Brackett was in no mood for *Digest* analogies. He was there to find Kemble, not salvation, and that in itself was startling enough. In all the years he had known his partner, he had never known him to dabble in religion, even in moments of crisis. Nevertheless he found Kemble after ten minutes, not in the synagogue but in the largest room of all, sponsored by the Church of Rome and decorated in California Gothic. He was kneeling in an empty pew, his shoulders hunched, staring at the altar. There was no mass, no priest to be seen. Kemble was merely praying. Or day-dreaming.

Brackett walked down the side-aisle, instinctively tip-toeing, until he reached Kemble's bench, glanced around self-consciously, then shuffled sideways until he was standing by Kemble's shoulder.

'Harry?' Brackett whispered.

There was no reaction. A priest appeared from a sacristy, caught Brackett's eye and nodded as if welcoming in a convert from the storm. Brackett caught himself nodding back and looked away.

'Harry?' he repeated a little louder, kneeling beside him and discovering he was still holding the comic books in his hand. He stared at them, then tried to slot them out of sight in a chair-rack designed for prayer books, but they fell out, scattering themselves (*Flash*, *Thor*, something called *The Swamp Thing*) noisily on to the floor. As Brackett stooped to pick them up, Kemble turned and looked at him.

'Walter. What are you doing here?'

'I came to see you.'

'Came to see me, eh? Well, that's nice of you, Walter.'

Brackett gave a brief smile and stared at the comics in his hand.

'I brought you these,' he said, suddenly wishing he was somewhere else.

'You came here just to give me some comics?'

Kemble was now studying Brackett, looking at him in a direct gaze. Brackett knew the look well, for he had seen Kemble employ it a hundred times when talking to evasive witnesses and the like. He had seen bravura reduced to a stammer, and men twice the size of Kemble flinch and prepare to sign away their soul.

'Well, not exactly, Harry . . .' Brackett said.

Kemble continued studying Brackett, watching his every move, the comics being twisted in his hands, a tic that had suddenly appeared on Brackett's face below the left eye. Aware of this, Brackett glanced away and for want of something to say gestured around the church:

'You know, Harry, I always thought you were Jewish.'

'It's quieter here.'

'Oh,' Brackett said. 'Don't they mind? I mean –'

'Walter, at my age, you've got to try for the accumulator.'

Brackett smiled self-consciously and was silent.

'What did you want, Walter?'

'Can we talk somewhere else? I mean it's difficult whispering. . .'

Kemble didn't reply for a moment then pointed to a confessional box in a corner near the altar. Two boxes divided by a grilled partition; one for the priest, one for the penitent.

'How about in there, Walter? Is that what you have in mind?'

'Well. . .'

'You look worried, Walter,' Kemble said. 'You really do. Something to do with a case you're on? One of our clients?'

'In a way.'

'Well, I'm always at your service, Walter.'

And Kemble grinned and repeated the pun as he gestured towards the confessional box. Brackett stood up and nervously walked down the side-aisle until he reached the curtained entrance. He walked fast, his mind attempting to phrase questions. Then he cautiously entered the darkened box, sat down and waited. The small wire grille was opposite him. He waited, feeling more relaxed in this sudden privacy until finally he heard the door opening on the other side of the partition, heard it close and a voice said:

'Forgive me, Father, for I have sinned.'

Brackett froze and stared blankly into the darkness. It wasn't Kemble's voice. It couldn't be.

'Harry, is that you?'

'It has been three weeks since my last confession, Father –'

'Wait a minute,' Brackett said anxiously. 'I think you're making a mistake.'

'I have made many mistakes, Father.'

'No, what I mean is – you've got the wrong idea.'

A stunned reply:

'I *have*?'

Brackett was about to answer but suddenly realized the absurdity of the situation and hurried out into the aisle. Kemble was still sitting calmly in the pew.

'Harry,' Brackett said, hurrying over to him and pointing back helplessly towards the confessional box. A puzzled face had now appeared, peering through the half-open door.

'Harry, I must talk to you –'

'Lower your voice, Walter. Mass is about to start.'

Brackett stared at Kemble in exasperation then slowly sat down on the pew. At the altar, the priest was selecting a page in a missal.

'Harry,' Brackett said finally. 'Maybe we can talk outside.'

'If there's anything on your mind, Walter, this is the best place in the world to worry it out.'

Brackett sighed and stared ahead of him. Someone in a nearby chapel was lighting a candle. By a pillar the latest encyclical was on sale for fifty cents.

'Are you thinking about Dorothy?' Kemble said, his voice kept to a whisper.

'No, I'm not thinking about Dorothy.'

'It's on my conscience, Walter. Your own wife.'

Brackett looked at him:

'No, Harry. That's forgotten. We agreed.'

'But it's on my conscience, Walter.'

Two rows in front, a man turned round and glared at them, then turned back, his neck reddening. Brackett ignored him.

'The doctor tells me you're –'

'You talked to the doctor?' Kemble said.

'Yes. Just now. I'm concerned about you. Your health. He says that you're fine. A-1.'

'He said that?'

'Yes. Look, can't we talk outside, Harry? I can't keep whispering like this.'

'It's too late, Walter. The gospel has started.'

As if to emphasize Kemble's remark, a bell rang and the congregation knelt. Brackett lowered himself on to the kneeler before him and leant closer to Kemble:

'He also says that he's pleased that you can drive now.'

'Who?'

'The doctor.'

Kemble stared at him then moved away.

'He shouldn't have told you that.'

'Why not? It's true, isn't it?'

'Yes...'

'Well then?'

'I wanted to surprise you, Walter.'

The congregation was now standing. Kemble and Brackett stood, then sat down.

'Harry?' Brackett said. 'Why didn't you tell me that you were well?'

'I said. I wanted to surprise you.'

'Is that the only reason?'

'No...'

'Tell me.'

'I thought if I told you, you wouldn't visit me any more.'

'What do you mean?'

'Everybody has visitors here. I like you visiting me. I look forward to it.'

'But Harry – if you can drive around, you could have visited *me*.'

'No, Walter. It's your office now. I wanted you to be – I wanted you to make it on your own. Don't you understand that, Walter? I wanted to see how you managed on your own. Without me. My protégé. Because that's what you are. And you didn't fail me.'

'Fail you?' Brackett said, raising his voice. He glared defiantly around him then lowered it and added: 'I lied to you, Harry. All the time. All those stories. I lied.'

'I'm not hearing you, Walter. My ears are closed. It's Sunday, Walter. Sunday.'

Brackett leant back and stared at his partner's face. He saw the eyes, the line of the mouth (the photograph on the wall slid into frame. Hands thumbing a champagne cork. The good old razzamatazz). The sign polished, the telephone dusted. The bound copies of *Black Mask*. That absurd bird from Malta.

'I said I lied to you, Harry. The clients. We could count them on the fingers of a mitten.'

'*Kyrie Eleison*. Know what that means?'

'Harry – did you lie to *me*? Apart from the car?'

'Lie to you?'

'Yesterday. Where were you yesterday?'

'I saw you yesterday.'

'I mean afterwards?'

Kemble was suddenly very still, remaining in profile.

'What do you want me to say, Walter?'

'The doctor said you were out all day.'

Brackett was now beginning to sweat despite the chilliness of the church. He tried to divorce himself from what was happening, tried to pretend that he was an observer. A fly on the wall. But he watched Kemble slowly turn his head and look at him and heard him say:

'If the doctor said I was out, then I must have been out. What more do you want me to say, Walter?'

Brackett stared at Kemble's face, at his eyes, then said:

'Nothing, Harry. Nothing.'

He stood up.

'Good-bye, Harry.'

'You will visit me again, won't you, Walter?'

Brackett didn't answer but moved along the bench and walked towards the door without looking back. He didn't tip-toe nor even attempt to be silent. Instead, as the Mass continued and all except Kemble stood up, Brackett threw open the door and then slammed it behind him. He could hear the noise reverberating around the building until he had reached the ground floor and was walking out on to the lawns. He could hear the sound, in fact, until he was twenty yards from the building but by that time his attention had been drawn by something else. Parked neatly between his Buick and the nearest cabana was a now-familiar black Ford sedan, its driver no longer clandestine but openly leaning against the bonnet and lighting a cigarette. It was Simmons.

'Why the hell have you been following me?' Brackett shouted, brushing aside the stares of doctors, patients and poker players. His frustration had now turned to anger and he was in no hurry to let it subside.

'I didn't realize you noticed,' Simmons replied calmly, placing the cigarette case in his pocket.

'Of course I damn well noticed. It *was* you last night, wasn't it?'

'Believe me, Brackett, you mustn't lose your temper. I only had your best interests at heart.'

'Go to hell,' Brackett replied and walked towards the Buick. As he did so he saw the police car parked on the other side of the gates, engine running, waiting. Brackett stopped, then said quietly:

'I assume that's not there for my benefit.'

Simmons didn't answer but simply folded his arms.

'Well,' Brackett said, glancing at the church, 'he's all yours. You even have a priest as a witness.'

He got into his car and slammed the door as the detective approached:

'Brackett –'

'Stay away from me, lieutenant, unless you want to arrest me too.'

Simmons shook his head and stood back and watched as the Buick moved fast towards the gates, out into the street, almost clipping the police car, then was gone. After a moment, Simmons walked slowly back to the Ford, put his hand on the roof, said:

'All right. Let's pick him up.'

Then got back into the car.

14

When Sidney Horowitz arrived at the room above Fatty's two hours later, he found Brackett sitting in a chair methodically tearing up files and sheets of paper and dropping them on to the floor. He stood at the door and watched, noticing the drawers pulled out of the desk and the waste-basket full to the brim. The telephone was off the hook and the framed photographs had been removed from the wall and were now standing face to the wardrobe.

Horowitz didn't say anything for a moment even though he was aware that Brackett knew he was in the room, then he stood by the window and stared down at the police car below.

'Simmons called you, then?' Horowitz said finally.

There was no answer.

'Walter – you don't have to take this so personally. How could you know.'

'Go away, Sidney.'

Horowitz didn't move.

'Well,' he said. 'At least it's over.'

Brackett looked up angrily:

'Is that all you can say?'

Brackett then fumbled among the papers until he found a bottle, upturned it, found it was empty and threw it across the room and watched it smash against the wall.

'Walter,' Horowitz said, suddenly concerned. 'It was *our* mistake, not yours. We should have begun with the girl right away. Then maybe we could have saved one life at least.'

'Sidney – will you fucking well get out of here!'

Horowitz hesitated.

'I'm sorry,' he said and began to move towards the door. 'I'm sorry . . . I'm not being very tactful.'

'Wait a minute,' Brackett said and turned around. 'I want to apologize as well.'

'You don't have to apologize to me, Walter.'

'I said I want to apologize to you and I *want* to apologize to you.' Brackett's voice was slurred and Horowitz glanced away self-consciously.

'I want to say I'm sorry,' Brackett continued. 'For what I thought about you. I'm sorry.'

'Walter, you don't have to explain. I understand.'

'No, you don't. No you fucking don't. No one does...'

Brackett had now found another bottle among the bedclothes and was filling up a glass.

'Fucking well don't...'

'Do you mind if I join you, Walter,' Horowitz said, emptying out a toothbrush from a tumbler.

Brackett shrugged:

'What have *you* got to be sorry for?'

'Well ... I don't think I'll make lieutenant any more. That's for sure...'

Brackett swayed slightly, blinked and looked at Horowitz.

'Why not?'

'Well, I should have followed up the lead. At the pound, remember? That was *my* job.'

Brackett stared at him, then slumped into the chair.

'So *I* did it for you. What the hell. The result's the same.'

'You could have got killed.'

'Hardeharhar. Isn't that what they used to say?'

'Walter, I don't understand why –'

'What are you doing with my fucking toothmug? Put my toothmug back.'

'I thought I'd have a drink with you.'

'I don't want you to. And I don't want your sympathy. Nor your fucking leek and potato soup.'

'Look, Walter,' Horowitz shouted, 'stop feeling sorry for yourself.'

'Where did you pick him up?' Brackett said. 'In the church or in the patio? Sitting in his little chair. Reading his little comics.'

'What?'

'Looking across the little lawns. Reading his little comics. Sitting on the patio.'

'He wasn't on the patio, Walter.'

'Well, in the church then. Stand up, sit down –'

'He wasn't in the church either. Didn't Simmons call you? He was in his den.'

'Harry doesn't have a den.'

'Who's talking about Harry?' Horowitz said startled. 'I'm talking about Plomer.'

Brackett looked up and stared blankly across the room.

'Who?'

'Plomer. Robert Plomer. Who the hell do you think I'm talking about?'

Brackett's mouth opened and he tried to rise, spilt some of the whiskey and sat down again.

'*Robert* Plomer?'

'Walter, I thought Simmons had called you... Didn't you know? The murderer was Plomer. He confessed.'

Brackett gaped, his mind scrambling to take everything in. *Plomer?* But of course. Plomer. On the side of the law. Billy Kent said that. With his private detectives and his nymphets. Plomer. Not Harry. Robert fucking Plomer.

'You're not fooling me, are you, Sidney?'

'Christ, no, Walter – I thought you *knew*. I thought the reason why you were quitting was because Simmons had called you. He wanted to give you hell for not telling him that you'd seen Plomer yesterday.'

'It was a gentleman's agreement.'

And then Brackett began to laugh.

'Plomer? What do you know? Have a drink, Sidney. Have two. Plomer. Jesus Christ. The Elk lawyer!'

'What's so funny?' Horowitz said.

'Plomer!'

'I've said that.'

'Yes. It had to be. It all fits. That's why Loomis recognized my card at the morgue. Because he'd seen it before. He probably stole the file for Plomer because Plomer knew the girl had been here. Clever fucker! Robert Pacific Avenue Plomer. Who would have known?'

Brackett grinned and poured another drink. Then his smile faded.

'*I* should have done,' he said finally as realization struck home. 'Me! That's who.'

Brackett stared out of the window at the street. He could see some children sitting on the Buick. He pressed his forehead against the wooden frame and closed his eyes. He was thinking of Kemble.

'Do you want another drink, Walter?'

'No...'

'Simmons thinks he probably didn't intend to kill the girl,' Horowitz said. 'But it happened and then everything snowballed. He was schizoid. His wife confirms that. So does his medical record. She suspected there was an affair but, well... You know, he was better informed about this city than we were. Even had private detectives. Contacts. Who knows what makes people how they are?'

'Why do you keep saying "was"?' Brackett asked.

'He committed suicide. That's how we found him. That was his confession in a way. He saw us arrive and went into his den and locked it. By the time we broke in, he was dead. No note but we found some polaroid shots of the girl.'

'He lied to me about that,' Brackett said. 'Well, he lied about everything. And I let him go. The big detective... Jesus, you really screwed this one up, didn't you, Walter Brackett?'

He moved away from the window and stared at the rubble around him. Conscious of Brackett's mood, Horowitz began to pick up some of the paper.

'Leave it, Sidney,' said Brackett. 'It makes no difference.'

'You can't blame yourself about Harry. We suspected him too.'

'But as Simmons said, you're paid to. I'm not.'

He walked to the door.

'Where are you going?' Horowitz asked.

'To see Harry. Maybe I can do something right. If it's not too late.'

Brackett opened the door, then stopped:

'Did you find out who Mary Malewski was? The girl?'

'No.'

'No idea at all?'

'No idea at all,' Horowitz said. 'Just somebody's sister.'

When Brackett arrived at Autumn Glades it was mid-afternoon. The lawns were deserted but this was probably, Brackett assumed, because most of the tenants would be resting. Taking a siesta. So too it appeared was Kemble, for the patio was empty and the door into the cabana closed.

Brackett knocked on one of the louvred panels, heard no answer, then entered.

'Harry?' he said cautiously and looked around. In the half-light, the room appeared very still, almost as if no one had ever lived in it. The cushions on the chairs were smooth, ashtrays clean and a pile of books was stacked neatly on a table as if waiting to be packed.

'Harry?' Brackett repeated, noting a trace of anxiety in his voice.

There was still no answer and Brackett quickly opened another door. It led into a bedroom, the bed stripped, blankets neatly piled at the end. Brackett turned and was about to leave when he saw Kemble. He had his back to him and was sitting motionless in a chair so that only the top of his head and a cigarette held in his right hand could be seen.

'Harry?' Brackett repeated, crossing the room. 'Why didn't you answer?'

Kemble still didn't move, but just remained sitting in the semi-darkness. Brackett reached the chair and looked down. His partner's eyes were closed as if he were sleeping. Brackett stared at him then slowly leant over to take the cigarette from Kemble's hand. As he picked it carefully from the fingers, he looked up. Kemble was staring at him, his eyes wide.

'Walter,' he said, his voice pleading, 'take me home. I don't want them to keep me in this place any more.'

The laughter became almost infectious as Brackett drove the Buick back towards San Francisco. It was the laughter of relief that the weekend was finally over, that everything was now all right. The future of both men would change, and in a way, their roles would be reversed. Kemble would be living above the delicatessen, maybe even open for business again (*But only in a small way, Walter. Got to realize one's limits*) while Brackett might even return to England.

'Take stock of my life, Harry. That's what you always told me to do.'

'Did I say that, Walter?'

'Yes, you did, Harry. All the time.'

Brackett smiled. He would miss San Francisco, he knew that. But he couldn't stay there any more, for it had outgrown him. The last two days had proved that, and though he never wanted to live through that nightmare again (and it *would* be a nightmare wherever he travelled) he was grateful that the experience had given him the humility to recognize himself for what he was worth. He regretted naturally that it hadn't happened fifteen years earlier, when Dorothy had been alive, but that was all in the past now. Fifty-three, after all, was not the end of the world. If he looked after himself.

'Turn the radio on, Walter,' Kemble said. 'I like the radio. Listen to it all the time.'

'I can't wait to see Liebermann when you enter the door,' Brackett said, selecting a local channel. Lazy Sunday music. 'He's kept your room just as you left it.'

'Liebermann has, eh? Does he still write those notes on wrapping paper?'

'The ones you can't read?'

'Yes. Those are the ones.'

Brackett laughed, then honked the car horn just for the hell of it. They were now driving south on the main highway into the city.

'I'll come and visit you, Harry. When I'm in town.'

'Not every Saturday?'

'No,' Brackett grinned. 'Not every – Hey!'

Brackett suddenly yelled and slammed on the brakes and said:

'Well I'll be damned.'

'What is it?' Kemble asked.

'I'll be damned.'

Kemble watched as Brackett opened the door and ran across the sidewalk towards a parking lot. He saw him shout, then he was out of sight for a moment, hidden by a billboard, and finally reappeared holding something in his arms. As he reached the car, Kemble saw that he was carrying a rather temperamental labrador.

'What the hell are you doing with that, Walter?'

'Mrs Markstein's dog,' Brackett replied as the labrador struggled to escape.

'What?'

'Mrs Markstein's – oh hold it for me will you, Harry?'

'Who's Mrs Markstein?'

'Just hold the fucking dog. I can't drive and –'

'Maybe I ought to sit in the back with it. Out of your way.'

'Yeah. All right.'

Kemble took the dog by the collar, stared at it puzzled, then settled into the back seat. Brackett sat behind the wheel, glanced back and grinned.

'He likes you.'

'Thanks,' Kemble replied without enthusiasm. 'So now will you tell me. Who's Mrs Markstein?'

'A client.'

'I thought you'd retired, Walter.'

'I have now.'

Brackett started the car and they drove in silence till they were approaching the Bay, and the familiar white buildings of the city could be seen on the skyline. The radio switched from music to a news summary headlining the end of the murder hunt and the suicide of Plomer. There was a brief interview with the police commissioner who was suitably modest and attributed all the credit to Simmons and Johanssen and a 'steadfast and unselfish dedication to uphold law and order'. Brackett was momentarily subdued, then glanced at the labrador that had now settled on Kemble's lap. He smiled as he pictured Mrs Markstein's face when he told her the good news and said out loud:

'You know, I think I'll hand over the dog on the way, Harry. It's just near Macy's. Maybe pick up a couple of bucks.'

In the back seat, directly behind Brackett, Kemble stared up at the russet girders of the Golden Gate Bridge and nodded:

'That's fine with me, Walter,' he said. 'But don't go round Union Square. You know how I hate those palm trees, Baby.'

The news bulletin was now replaced by a jingle for cakemix but Brackett didn't hear it. He didn't hear anything except Kemble's words. He almost said *What fucking palm trees?* but he didn't.

Naturally he was conscious of the cars scrambling to brake behind him as he stopped the Buick in the centre lane and switched off the ignition. He was also conscious of Kemble smiling at him in the rear view mirror, an expression of almost parental pride as if Brackett had just graduated with honours. A man in shirtsleeves suddenly wrenched open the car door and asked him what the hell he was doing parking his car on the Golden Gate Bridge and that if he didn't move he'd call the cops. Brackett slowly raised his head and looked at the man and then said quietly:

'Why don't you do that?'

As the man swore and hurried away, Brackett turned and without looking at Kemble leant over the seat, picked up the labrador and got out of the car. As he was closing the door he heard Kemble say:

'You will still visit me, won't you, Walter? Like you always did?'

Brackett stopped and stared at Kemble for a long time, then shook his head.

More about Penguins and Pelicans

Penguinews, which appears every month, contains details of all the new books issued by Penguins as they are published. From time to time it is supplemented by *Penguins in Print*, which is our complete list of almost 5,000 titles.

A specimen copy of *Penguinews* will be sent to you free on request. Please write to Dept EP, Penguin Books Ltd, Harmondsworth, Middlesex, for your copy.

In the U.S.A.: For a complete list of books available from Penguins in the United States write to Dept CS, Penguin Books, 625 Madison Avenue, New York, New York 10022.

In Canada: For a complete list of books available from Penguins in Canada write to Penguin Books Canada Ltd, 2801 John Street, Markham, Ontario L3R 1B4.

Lionel Davidson

Smith's Gazelle

On one level Lionel Davidson's book is an enchanting fairy story about a small boy from a kibbutz and an ancient Arab joined together in their determination to rescue a beautiful species of gazelle from extinction.

On another level it is the compelling kind of adventure story his readers expect.

Making Good Again

In Germany to settle a claim for reparation, lawyer James Raison is plunged into the old conflict between Jew and Nazi. His trip becomes more dangerous as the legal aspects of the case become more complicated and at the same time he has to cope with his affair with Elke and his fascination for her fascist mother Magda...

The Night of Wenceslas

Young man-about-town Nicolas Whistler, whose father had once had an interest in a Bohemian glassworks, really had no choice when he was suddenly 'invited' to make a business trip to Prague. Happily there was said to be no danger in the journey: Nicolas was no hero. But he becomes more and more deeply engulfed in the seamy underworld of power politics.

Penguin also publish three other books by Lionel Davidson:

A Long Way to Shiloh
The Rose of Tibet
The Sun Chemist

Paul Theroux

The Great Railway Bazaar

Fired by a fascination with trains that stemmed from childhood, Paul Theroux set out one day with the intention of boarding every train that chugged into view from Victoria Station in London to Tokyo Central, and to come back again via the Trans-Siberian Express.

And so began a strange, unique and hugely entertaining railway odyssey.

'In the fine old tradition of purposeless travel for fun and adventure . . . compulsive reading'
– Graham Greene

'One of the most entertaining books I have read in a long time . . . superb comic detail' – Angus Wilson in the *Observer*

The Family Arsenal

A novel of urban terror and violence set in the grimy decay of South-East London.

'One of the most brilliantly evocative novels of London that has appeared for years . . . very disturbing indeed' – Michael Ratcliffe in *The Times*

'An uncomplicated pleasure . . . with this writer the thrills are never cheap and obvious' – Robert Nye in the *Guardian*

'Mr Theroux has the ability to turn the familiar into the fabulous' – Francis King in the *Sunday Telegraph*

Derek Marlowe

Do You Remember England?

Who is Dowson?

'When he left on the Sunday – the others had gone to visit Aunt Beth's rose garden (plus *bosquet*) and returned to find his room empty – there were no regrets . . . he had stayed thirty-six hours, had glimpsed Hallam's wife only for a second . . . and I knew that nothing could ever be the same again.'

'This is an ingenious and elegant novel about two perfect people . . . the book is an elegy, intricately constructed and written, for youth and beauty, for the past long ago' – *Books and Bookmen*

Nightshade

A trip to the Caribbean takes Edward and Amy to Haiti, a place of unaccountable fear and peculiar coincidence.

Paradise turns to hell, the hell of Baron Samedi, the voodoo lord of death.

'Derek Marlowe's *Nightshade* is a genuinely weird book . . . his sensibility is freakishly his own' – Jill Neville

Derek Marlowe

A Dandy in Aspic

' "You're not an English dandy, Eberlin. You're not even a loyal English gentleman. You know what you are?"

"Tell me," said Eberlin quietly.

Gatiss looked at Eberlin's face steadily. "An assassin," he said.'

A Dandy in Aspic is the story of a man ordered to Berlin to track down and kill a ruthless Russian assassin and double agent, Krasnevin. A difficult assignment, since he himself is Krasnevin.

The Disappearance

Jay's wife is missing. He's offered four times his usual rate to kill a man called Feather. He dithers. Goes places. Searching for Celandine, dodging his assignment, running into trouble.

A contact is killed. Friends blur into foes. More and more it looks like Jay's last job...

The Disappearance is a tense, close-knit triumph in which Derek Marlowe deploys highly wrought thriller tactics to X-ray the soul of a man whose cynicism has hardened into an arctic despair.